750

GW00786489

pegasus in the suburbs

Jennifer Kremmer grew up in south-western Sydney and studied at Newcastle and UTS. She currently lives in Campbelltown and is planning a novel about presentation aesthetics, body image and waste. *Pegasus in the Suburbs* is her first novel.

pegasus
in the
suburbs

Jennifer Kremmer

ALLEN & UNWIN

First published in 1999 by
Allen & Unwin
9 Atchison Street,
St Leonards NSW 1590 Australia
Phone: (61 2) 8425 0100
Fax: (61 2) 9906 2218
E-mail: frontdesk@allen-unwin.com.au
Web: http://www.allen-unwin.com.au

National Library of Australia
Cataloguing-in-Publication entry:

Kremmer, Jennifer.
  Pegasus in the suburbs.

  ISBN 1 86508 001 2.

A823.3

Set in 10.5/13pt Palatino by DOCUPRO, Sydney
Printed by Australian Print Group, Maryborough, Victoria

10 9 8 7 6 5 4 3 2

Thanks to my parents, to Margie & Richie, and to Belinda, Gary & David. Special thanks to fellow workers at CPSU.

For my mother, father, sisters and brother, and growing up in the sticks.

Crush

ONE

Maree became a girl before she could be anything else.

As a girl, she thought the only thing worse than being born a girl was to be born unlucky. Later she knew that there is no such thing as luck.

Being born is just being born.

Being a girl is being taught to be a girl.

Her mother bought her a trainer bra. The trainer bra sat on the bed because Maree refused to try it on. The trainer bra was pink.

Every day, Maree's mother said, 'Have you tried on that bra I bought you?'

Every day, Maree said, 'What, that stupid old thing, it can rot on my bed for all I care. I don't need one. If I ever get boobs I'll have them cut off. I'll never have a baby anyway.' And she would turn back to a drawing she was doing on the kitchen table, among cereal packs and jam jars and her mother's bits of unfinished or forgotten sewing, packs of press-studs and cotton reels, discarded broken needles and half-moons of fabric from the offcuts of sleeves.

Her mother was always running things up, putting them on, picking them undone. She was always saying to Maree or her older sister Lissa, 'Come here and try this,' with pins in her lips.

Maree thought of her mother as a woman who spoke through pins.

Between them was the idea of shape. Maree's mother spent hours cutting shapes from fabric. She fed the fabric into the sewing machine so that the fabric would fit her children's bodies. This was because she wanted to shape the bodies of her children, which for her were the body she had lost when somehow she had stopped being, or being allowed to be, a girl.

Thus, since it was her own girlish body she was fitting clothes for, it was hard to make the clothes fit others. Maree's mother was constantly throwing things away.

For Maree, shape meant the end of everything. She wanted to be up-and-down straight, like a line. Like a ruler. She wanted this because to have shape was to be a target, exactly like a bullseye. Living targets walked around waddling and encumbered. Even Lissa was developing shape.

Maree had to be watchful. At thirteen, spindle-limbed and skittish, she had what's called the eye.

To describe it was like this: 'Look out for that moll, Johnno, she's got the eye!'

Although she didn't know what a moll was, Maree blushed. She blushed because she was embarrassed to be caught looking, even by accident. Looking was what caused skirmishes, the skirmishes that caused war. Looking was provocation. Maree was doomed.

Sometimes on the bus coming home from school, boys

would point at Maree or Lissa. When they pointed at Lissa, they said, 'Show us your pussy, Fancy-pants,' or, 'Come and meet Mr Pink.' The boys laughed. They targeted Maree's sister constantly. To avoid showing that she minded, or perhaps because she did not mind, Maree's sister was always blushing and smiling. Blushing and smiling were like two open hands. They were the palm-out gestures of peace.

When boys looked at Maree, it was in dismay. They said, 'Moll's got an earache.' Or they said, 'Where's sis?'

Everything about boys was different to everything about girls. This was the way the world worked.

One day, Maree was playing with the children of her father's workmates, called, for the sake of respect, cousins. As she ran around the perimeter of an above-ground pool, she came upon one of her cousins crouched between the stanchions. His name was Pilar and he thought he was safe. He was crouching so that he could peer every now and then over the top of the pool.

Maree had a plastic pistol in her hand and she pointed it right at her cousin and said, 'Gotcha!' exactly as the boys did when they played. She pointed the pistol and imitated the sound of gunfire as though such sounds routinely exploded in her mouth.

But Pilar continued looking around the stanchion for other boys. He did not pretend to have been hit.

She said, 'Hey, I shot you.'

'Who cares?' He did not even look at her.

Maree realised that boys were different because only the actions of other boys mattered to them. Making the rules, they alone knew how to ignore them.

In the playground, because she was a younger sister, Maree was shy. She was a lamb in a zoo of predators. To survive in the playground with the carnivores, Maree saw that it was necessary to flee. She was always walking around corners watching the sky for missiles.

If she walked too close to a handball game, the ball would pelt like lightning into the space of her walking, as sharp and hot as a bullet. She would clutch her stinging leg and say, 'Oof!' Then she would have to pretend that the spot the ball had smacked was somewhere safe toward her knee or lower calf, rather than somewhere vital, such as up on her thigh. Up high, boys might say, 'Aargh, got Sterry in the cunt!' Low, they might look away.

In any case, she fled.

Maree turned from the playground and from boys. She invented a world because the world of inventions seemed fuller than the world in which she was a moll. The world of inventions was safe.

Once, Maree was walking behind her mother through a park near a churchyard lined with clothes racks and appliances. The proximity of clothes with their shapely suggestions made her mother say, 'Wait here.'

Maree slouched against a mesh fence, watching people browse. A bulky woman in a floral dress smiled at her across the top of a knitting stall. Embarrassed, Maree scowled. She did not specifically mean to slouch or scowl, but she was adolescent.

A bearded animal, or perhaps a man, sat on a deck chair in front of a lime-green panel van. Beside him were rows of paintings of women with long hair that became manes of horses, and vice versa. Horses that became the manes of long women. The horses' eyes were dark-rimmed and haunted. Their frosty necks arched whitely and their chest muscles bulged like hillocks. She felt thrilled, as though she could feel the warm arch of the animals' spines and the thrumming of their muscular ribs.

Maree was aware while looking at the paintings that the man's thonged feet crossed and recrossed upon each other. This made her feel that she was being watched. So that she did not notice the man, so that she would not have to meet his watchful eyes, Maree kept her gaze on the paintings.

TWO

The difference between Maree and her mother was that her mother knew that Maree would cease to be a girl. Maree's mother knew this because it had happened to her, a long time before Maree was born or became an adolescent.

When Maree's mother was much younger, she lost her parents. Perhaps they died in a war or perhaps they just did not come home. At any rate, Maree's mother was left an orphan. This was how she became a non-girl. Out in the world, all a girl can do is grow up. There is nobody to reassure her that childhood is possible. There is nobody to tell lies.

Therefore childhood disappears. *Phoof*.

Put into an orphanage, Maree's mother had been alone in the world. Being alone in the world, she was ever nostalgic for a time in which she had briefly been a girl in a marriage of father and mother, like a Nativity scene. In a common imaginary, it was not natural to be alone in the world; it was as though nobody saw that Nativity scenes were fabrications of a lost ideal. Not knowing how society operated, Maree's mother pined for this diorama all the way through her young life until she met a man, Maree's father, and signed his name on a contract. The contract replaced her name, which was the name of her father, with the name of a new father.

Diorama.

Nativity.

Years later she was folding laundry when she recalled having once been a girl. This was such a foolish recollection that she cried.

Since girlhood had disappeared for Maree's mother, she often looked at her three girls, Lissa, Maree and the late-born infant Samantha, and thought, Fools. Simpletons. She thought that each of her girls was in for a shock.

Because Maree's mother's thoughts were shocking, she had to keep them to herself. In the Sterry family, in the family name, she dusted the panes, waxed floors, emptied the vacuum cleaner and applied anti-mould products to the bathroom tiles. Between major modifications she drifted from room to room, opening and closing curtains, picking up shoes. She devoted entire afternoons to the unpicking of strategic seams on old clothes, to turn them into door-jamb dusters or cleaning cloths. It was impossible to say what she thought. Once a door-knocking salesman winked at her through the venetian blinds. Maree's mother, standing against the window, whisked them closed. Lines from the venetians striped her expression. She did not move.

Maree could not understand her mother because nothing she learned at school had anything to do with motherhood. At school the girls learned maths, English, geography, science, art and a version of history. Lissa, being studious, also learned how to sew and cook and how to fold paper napkins so that they resembled butterflies or swans. But these latter skills were insignificant, like the practices of washing and mending shirts. They were the accoutrements of mothering, not its essence.

Lacking information, Maree's ideas grew wild. She read in a nature encyclopaedia that stoats will allow their young to eat their own flesh if food is scarce. The idea repelled her, but it helped to explain the look on Mrs Sterry's face as she served the children their evening meals.

Perhaps Maree was wrong, and her mother was happy to be a mother. It was impossible to know given the nature of the family. Nobody could take Mrs Sterry aside and ask her how she felt, since they were all equally a part of the family and equally prone to its rules and anomalies, its protection and disregard. To any of them, it just seemed that Mrs Sterry was so fixed in the home she had no duration outside of it. When they were with her, she existed; when they were not, she did not. Nobody thought to ask whether she was happy.

In fact, everybody forgot Mrs Sterry when they were away from her. Lissa kissed boys behind the weather sheds. Samantha put her fingers into spiderwebs. Maree drew pictures in the dirt and fled from passers-by, yelling rudely. Their father tinkered with the car, and once was hurled backward from a blue electric spark. He said, 'Kids, my life flashed before my eyes and I wondered who would look after you all.' That their father imagined only he looked after them was indicative of his place and time, and not that he was a cruel or thoughtless man. In the Sterry house, in the Sterry suburb, nobody noticed what mothers were about.

In response to the fact that she did not exist for her

family whenever they left her space, Mrs Sterry took to disappearing when they were present. She brushed by them indifferently, like a ghost. She rarely spoke. It was as though by self-annihilation, by absence, she could provoke them into a kind of regard.

This was anything but the stoat feeding her flesh to her brutal young. It was a sort of dispute, though it had no negotiating table and only the vaguest list of demands. It was just Maree's mother wishing for a different world.

In absentia, Mrs Sterry smoked and read books. She had a method of disposing of cigarette butts by first rinsing them under the tap, then tucking each soggy stub into the dark recess of the kitchen-tidy bin. At each disposal she would grimace to either side of her in sudden self-consciousness and jerk like a wind-up toy. All actions for her were preactions. She lived in a defensive present, preoccupied by a nostalgic past. She feared her own disappearance as much as she craved it.

Preoccupied with absence, Maree's mother danced after insects, filming surfaces with Mortein, coating tongues and nasal passages and hairs on arms. Weeding the garden, she was brutal. Around her flies spun on their backs on the windowsills, or dropped from mid-air onto tiles, waving spindly legs.

It was possible to tell that their mother had been in a room by the dwindling source of a buzz.

The children went from room to room, waving their hands in front of their watering eyes. They did not know what to do with their mother, supposing something had to be done. They did not know the meaning of setting the table or of considering what to cook. All they knew was to be prepared when their father was due home.

One day, Maree put the washing out on the line. Her

mother, smoking, watching from the back step, said, 'Don't put too many socks out at once. Don't hang the shirt upside down. Put the red towel up by itself.'

Above them, sparrows found new twittering places as the neighbour's trimmer whirred. Maree's mother, half a sparrow herself, looked to the sky. In her face was a strange look of envy. Perhaps she wished she could fly.

In the evenings, the mother satisfied the requirements for her family's nutrition by providing meals with the unhappy aplomb of a bowling-club chef. She swatted the tablecloths and covered exposed arms with mosquito repellent to spare them itchy bites and passed more gravy when the hands clamoured. She said, 'What?' suspiciously if glanced at out of the blue; crossed both arms and was visibly relieved if left alone.

Maree came across a photo of her mother holding Lissa, then a baby, in a white baby rug. The picture showed a smiling-faced woman with pulled back hair and a shiny nose. She was laughing to the camera. Her face was curved and lineless. Her cheeks were pink, exactly the colour of Maree's trainer bra. It was as though her mother had once been happy, like a woman in a margarine ad.

This reminded Maree of the last time her mother had laughed. Maree had been colouring in a picture of a pony when her mother suddenly squealed at a breadcrumb in her cup of tea. Her father had shrugged with a guilty look.

'Oh, you, you,' their mother cried. Maree and Lissa gazed, slack-mouthed.

Their mother began throwing cushions at their father's head. Lissa rattled the venetian edges in disquiet; the neighbours might hear. Their father ducked each tossed cushion, but sweeps of his hair grew ragged and he looked like an escapee or a crazy musician. He reached under the recliner rocker and found a thong, which he slapped against his palm, saying, 'Oh, yeah, you wanna start something, woman?' His language shocked Maree, and she went up the hall to hide.

Lissa joined her and said, 'Mum and Dad have gone mad.' Together the young girls went into their shared bedroom. They could hear the bumps and scrapes of their parents' tumble and, finally, the slamming of a door.

Nine months later, Samantha had been born. The youngest girl was the product of either the slammed door or her mother's laughter, it was hard to decide. Perhaps happiness caused kids and regret. At any rate, their mother had never laughed again, or if she had it was quietly, to herself.

Occasionally their father would gaze at Samantha fondly and say, 'That was some breadcrumb and some cup of tea, eh Missus?' In the room behind him Mrs Sterry would snort or blush. Yet she loved her last born daughter most of all. That was the paradox, it seemed, of motherhood.

In the wild, stoats fed their flesh to baby stoats. Motherhood was about self-sacrifice. Whether she had wanted a third child or not, Maree's mother kept quiet about how she felt.

In many ways, the Sterry family approximated a corporation. Their mother was an ancient employee, not understood, though tolerated. She supplied the toast and tea and best utilised the funds that their father gave her to house and clothe them. She was the only worker willing to perform certain age-old functions yet nobody remembered to consult her.

In the Sterry family, the mother went without so that her children could go clad. Hence she sometimes looked shabby. There was a fine line between self-sacrifice in the pursuit of family goals and a public statement of the meagreness of family profit margins, which Maree's mother sometimes crossed, or meandered obliviously or wilfully toward.

One afternoon, when there was a bus strike, she picked the children up from school, scarf around her head and the blue family Ford with its one pink door making a shimmying whirr. Scarcely looking at Lissa or Maree, she snapped, 'Come on, hop in, I haven't got all day.' Her dress was an old gown tied up with cord, and her feet on the brake pedals were clad in grey sheepskin. She looked a sight, a fright. A panic.

Fortunately for Maree and Lissa, each acutely conscious of the potential for schoolyard taunts, their mother was quick to depress the accelerator pedal. They were lucky to get home alive.

Lissa, storming into the bedroom, said, 'I hate the way that woman dresses.'

Maree, jumping, looked to see that her mother had not heard.

When one of the girls spoke to their mother, she often forgot to look up. She was often busy. If she was not ironing, she was cooking. If she was not cooking, she was cleaning. If she was not cleaning, she was watching TV or smoking cigarettes.

She often smoked in the lounge room, feet on a pouffe. When they said, 'Mum', she looked away. It was as though whatever they were saying could not possibly be to her, was just a murmur in the walls.

If they persisted, she would suddenly stare up and through them, as though they did not exist, even though they were asking her something ordinary like 'Where did you put the tomato sauce?' She would point to a cupboard as though it were just something she did in answer to a murmur in the walls, supposing walls might murmur.

In the meantime, she sewed seams so that those seams were invisible. She mended coats so that they appeared new. She stitched the family emblem onto the collars of jumpers and cardigans. Sometimes she forgot her own appearance, but she never forgot her new name, or signed a form, accidentally or otherwise, with the old one.

On the television, infant elephants trumpeted for their poached mamas, tracking their trunk-ends through the bloodied dust. Female chimpanzees climbed the rafters of jungles, fighting the clutches of overbrawned males for the rag-doll bodies of their babies. The only thing to do was avoid maternity.

Maree took to examining herself for bumps on her chest. She read books in which heroines were smart and slim. She began sucking her cheeks into her face to try to develop an angular look. She scurried about the house in fear of her mother, afraid of becoming one.

Maree once watched a race on television. Eleven horses lined up for the starting bell. The favourite was a mare. She had long legs, sound wind, high head carriage and sure hooves. She pounded past the heavy-crested stallions and spiritless geldings.

When she was past winning, she would become a brood mare.

Despite everything, it seemed that motherhood was fate.

THREE

The Sterry family was like a new branch in Darwinian logic. Suburban, nuclear, it was the outcome of its time. Everything that had gone into producing it was reflected in the architecture and space, the suburb. To maintain the illusion of consequence, driveways led from houses onto roads, and roads from the suburb to elsewhere. Cars waited at kerbsides or on driveways. The driving of cars was not necessarily always masculine, but a mirror was often tucked behind the passenger seat visor. It was the perfect height and width to apply lipstick.

The Sterry family had arrived like a birth into a space already crowded with expectations. They did not invent brick veneer or Pebblecrete, but somehow these materials and methods flourished. Behind brick skins, radiata pine carried structure, exactly like a stage set. Yet to look at, these houses resembled solid brick.

Around the Sterrys, suburbia mushroomed. Vacant blocks were filled in like gapped teeth, leaving miracles of new construction and parked cars. In fact, these homes were mostly filled with air, in the porousness of brick as well as in the spaces above ceiling joists and underneath the floors. Nobody cared as long as they could choose between bamboo wallpaper, pastels and featured brick for the interior walls.

Beyond the space of suburbia was the idea of the city: the teacher at the front of a class slapping a ruler onto the desk so the children would pay attention. As teacher, the city could send the bad kids out to see the principal, to the suburbs. It was a bit like England and the colonies.

So that, despite the presence of Family, which oversaw all, the suburbs were full of unruly students, the hotbeds of unrest. The bad students were made to sit at the back of the classroom so that they would not continually disrupt the process of learning. Even so, they were always interrupting or exploding waterbombs or lifting the skirts of girls with the curved ends of hockey sticks.

Maree's family struggled to hear what was said. Listening among the unruly students, they lip-synched in a greater effort to acquire knowledge. Because they were busy lip-synching, they believed unreflectively what they were told; there was no time to reflect. There was only time to absorb.

It was easy to see in the fact of their very distance from the city, being removed from its whirling life, a sort of security. Streets all led somewhere else; there was a central vista, a point of greatest purview. Somebody was taking care of things.

The Sterry family was always looking out for something else. They believed in this something else as an alter-ego to themselves. It was the something else that spun the threads of illumination along the highways and made hot water for their showers and pictures for night-time TV. It was the something else that gave a point to all their labours, to the industrious lino-scrubbing of Maree's scarved mother, on her hands and knees, and to the tight-frowned entry through the front door of Maree's father, divested of his daily work and yet not quite untasked, because there were always children to order, a family to control.

Maree's mother was perhaps less convinced of the presence of the something else with its possibilities, but still she scrubbed. Despite scrubbing, dust built up in corners, consisting of asbestos particles, fly parts, hair, skin cells and lead. To the touch, it resembled fairy floss.

Their father was the centre of the family, its nucleus. He was like radiation, neither felt nor seen, but experienced. Being like the sun, he shone and devastated with equal radiance. He gave them sunburn and holidays. He once said to Maree, 'Do not even *think* what you were going to say.' Maree, having not yet thought of what she was going to say, could only comply.

Even the grass appeared to flourish under his rays. He loved his charges. He was the centre of their particular universe, oversaw everything in it. By the time Maree and her sisters were old enough to doubt, they did not doubt him; they doubted the world. They doubted themselves in the constancy of the house.

Because they doubted themselves, it was not in any of the Sterry children to wonder about their position in the house. Yet as tenants, they had no rights. Law gave the children to the parents and the wife to the husband. War-torn faces littered the television; news provided comparisons that made even the children's rightless tenancy seem fortunate.

Pegasus in the Suburbs

This was why every house had a television.

Their father had brought one home when Maree was very small. It was as though he wanted to show them his creations. It was his way of saying, 'See?' If it contradicted his wishes, he could always switch it off.

Once it was in place, in its rightful centre of the lounge room, their mother watched it to take herself from the absence of herself. Or perhaps she watched to remind herself why she felt out of place. The television was a machine for supplying the excess of information necessary for the erasure of memory.

Watching, she folded washing. Folding washing, Maree's mother often found her memory erased.

At or after dinnertime, Maree's father would sit squarely in front of the set in his recliner rocker, where he would shift back and forth until he had settled and then his gaze would drift onto the screen. Rocket launches would duplicate on the glassy balls of his eyes. It was impossible to imagine what he thought.

If Maree said, 'Dad' repeatedly, he would turn without peeling his eyes from the screen and say, 'What the hell do you want?' or 'Hang on a minute, love,' depending on his mood. Maree sometimes watched her father watching television. She saw the flickers and nuances in his expressions as the balls of various sports were whacked, bowled or kicked. Often he seemed to be imagining what he would say to the man next to him in the aisle seat.

It was once important to Maree that she be allowed to view a horse movie. Her father was watching highlights of a rugby match he'd already seen. Maree dithered in the background, wringing her hands. She fretted silently. It was time to change the channel. Time to change it. Go on, Dad, it's time to change the channel. Time. To. Change channel.

Finally she said, 'Dad, *National Velvet*'s on.'
He looked at her, his expression glazed. 'Wha?'
'National Velvet.'
He turned back to the screen and said, 'Well, why don't you flick it across then? These are just highlights, love.'

The movie had already started. She watched the opening sequences around the bulky figure of her father, who had remained standing in the middle of the room with his arms crossed.

Evenings were muted at the edges of the lounge room, where terry towelling and laundered flannelette filled the space with their airy fibres. The family inhaled themselves—each other, food remnants, sweat, and the fibres of their clothes—with every breath. The only distance possible was on the other side of the news and its offshoots, out of the invisible rays of television. Or, upon first chancing into the room, before the narrative had filtered into the sense-making portions of the brain. While casting about the room for a comfortable chair, it was sometimes possible to halt and say, 'What on earth is this?'

If ever such a question were asked, whoever was watching would spin abruptly and say, 'Wha?'

The nuclear family was an accident of geography, bureaucracy, climate, shipping timetables, genetics and technological advancement. Nobody living in one was to blame, least of all the centrepiece Mr Sterry, who, having been forced to 'make' himself, did the best he could with the materials at hand. Because of geography, climate, bureaucracy and shipping timetables he did not know where his parents were, only that they were in another country. Because of technological advancement, which placed him definitively within a work role that took away his time even to continue to make himself, he did not have the leisure to pursue enquiries.

Because of genetics, he was just a man in a physical situation. He could not know things that were beyond his scope to see or know.

He had not seen his parents since he was twelve. They had sent him out to work one day with an uncle because they were too continually drunk to go on caring for him, then they had abandoned him and gone overseas or inter-state. After being forgotten by his parents, Maree's father arrived in a suburb. He bought a car, met Maree's mother, married her, and had her change her name to something that seemed more natural: his.

His parents became a memory of twin breasts and a false, knowing look. Between them were desert, air, sea-water, rock and memories, both false and real. These were the inexplicabilities of Maree's father's prior life.

Because of its lost grandparents, the family was more nuclear than most. In a way, it was super-nuclear. With only scraps and shrapnel of their ancestry they had no collective recollections. They were born into the shadow of a father bigger than God, seeing all, knowing all.

The family name was their father's logo. His name made them isolated, different: the Sterrys versus the rest of the world. Their father often said, 'I don't mind if you marry a Negro or Chinaman. I don't care if he's Protestant, if he smokes, if he votes Liberal or if he fought in the Boer War. All I care about is that my daughters grow into decent young women who do the right thing.'

Replace 'right' with 'Sterry'.

To keep them in place, he withheld pocket money when they failed to work. He supplied them with sporting meta-phors to maintain a spirit of progress, or the spirit of a spirit of progress. The idea of the spirit of a spirit. Of progress.

He bought the television and a car, an unremarkable blue Ford Falcon station wagon which now had one pink-undercoated door. Their father had had to undercoat the door because it came from a different car and was the wrong colour. He had had to buy a car door of the wrong colour because the original door had been swept off when their mother had opened it in front of a school bus. He had never gotten around to repainting the car because he did not wish to spend money on a vehicle that he would one day sell. Suburbia was about finding lulls in which to concoct schemes, only to see those schemes fall away. Time in surburbia was never expansive enough.

Their mother had been parking the car because their father had come home from work early and had agreed to let her use it to do some shopping. Nobody knew why she had flung the door open in front of the bus, nor why the bus, just sweeping around the corner, had not taken a wider arc.

Maree had been on the bus at the moment of impact. She had been standing, ready to alight at her stop. Time had actually frozen in alarm. Other kids on the bus were waving their anemone arms, momentarily silenced. Goggle-eyes watched her sway toward the bus steps.

The bus driver, a small man like a monkey, got off in front of her, scratching his head. He did not seem to know what to do. When children on the bus were unruly he would occasionally stall the engine and sit there ticking until the children sensed his annoyance and gradually, even the most troublesome of them, grew quiet. Then he would start up again and continue on the route.

Specifics like the hurling into his path of unruly doors were not in his repertoire of mishaps.

Maree, schoolbag in hand, watched as her mother dissolved in tears and began wailing onto the bus driver's shoulder. She was crying, 'Oh, he'll . . . he'll kill me, he'll k-k-kill me.'

The bus driver looked to be about half her size.

On the bus, the schoolchildren saw what was happening and wolf-whistled.

Maree tried to walk up her driveway as though the woman at the kerb by the car with one sawn-off door and the bus driver standing sheepishly in an embrace of empathy were connected to somebody else, perhaps the neighbour or a household down the road.

But the other kids were beginning to recognise Maree's mother, or to make, in the unerring way children have, correct assumptions. As a second bus pulled up to take the remaining children to their respective stops, Maree hid behind the lounge-room venetians, where she heard the calls of boys from school. 'Sterry, Sterry, who's got the ball? See I haven't, see I haven't, who's got the ball?' and 'Sterry's mum and the bus driver sitting in a tree, k-i-double s-i-n-g.'

This was a new moment in her parents' life as parents; as people whose union had produced new and unruly occurrences, like kids and mishaps. They took to banging doors and snapping at each other after lengthy silences.

Maree's father walked between laundry and garage saying, 'Stupid bloody woman can't drive, can't even look out for a damn bus.' He would have pulverised a sparrow with a wrench had the sparrow sat on the paling cheeping at him for a moment longer. He believed that even a sparrow could be out to deride him and his family, his torture, his missing driver's side door.

Had it been the *passenger* side door, he might well have forgiven her. But the driver's was his side, and he fumed.

Maree's mother took to looking through blinds and curtains, as though hoping for another bus that would take her away, out of here. She became ghost-pale and busied herself with macramé, knotting long webs as obscurely purposeful as nooses. When their father walked into the kitchen, she would get up to stack the dirty dishes.

She hung pot-plants in the macramé webs outside doors and windows so that family members, looking up at a startling noise as they played with a hose or dug in the dirt, would bounce their heads against the heavy-soiled plastic and wonder, suddenly, where and what on earth they were.

The car sat at the kerb, doorless, until their father taped the driver's side with a sheet of industrial plastic and set about trying to fix it. He welded a new hinge joint onto the door frame. This took hours of welding and filing and eventually had to be redone properly at a panel-beater's shop. He took the damaged door to a wrecker's yard and bought another one of the wrong colour for thirty dollars. Then he noticed that the new door's hinge was damaged as well, and had to take it into the garage to have it straightened.

When he hit it too hard, the hinge snapped. He was back to square one.

He began to weld the hinge.

Maree, empathising with her father because of her embarrassment over her mother's mistake and at the same time curious, stood shyly in her father's garage passing him metal files or welding rods. Since she tried so hard, her father could not help but approve. His daughter was turning into Daddy's girl.

Every time he said, 'Look away,' she turned aside and felt the blue sparks melt in her hair. Had she looked into the light, she would have been blinded, for her father was as fierce as the sparks.

One morning, Maree stood in front of the bathroom mirror trying to part her hair evenly with a comb. Cow-licks made the parting a struggle not unlike the struggle of her mother every day to untangle washing mangled in the machine. Maree, struggling, felt as unhappy and wet as the tangled clothes, or the look on the tangled and mangling face of her mother.

Just then, her father walked past down the hall.

'Dad,' she called out, 'can I start wearing short socks? Everybody at school does.'

Long socks were her father's idea of what a girl wore. He stuck his head inside the bathroom door. 'Why do you want to wear short socks to school? Is it just because everybody wears them? What are you, some sort of sheep? Do you have to follow the herd?'

He wanted the best for his children, hence he gave them the best rules. One of these was that they must be individuals, capable of spontaneous self-assertion. It chagrined him when they were not. Yet he loved his daughters so much that he was constantly hugging them against his tan work shirt, cracking their shoulder bones hard into their sockets, or patting their heads violently as he passed.

Their mother, who was often appalled by his approaches and incensed by his familiarity, called out, 'Let her wear short socks if she wants to, for God's sake.'

In the bathroom, Maree slumped, staring into the mirror. She had not meant to cause major disruption. She was wondering what was wrong with her family, or what was wrong with the world that only permitted the wearing of long socks up to a certain age, or what was wrong with her, since she must be the only person in the world who had to ask her father's permission to change. Perhaps her father was right. What was wrong with long socks, anyway? They covered the shins. They kept down the hairs. They protected a gangly part of Maree from the view of the world. It had only been the hectoring of other children that had made an issue of long socks.

Her sister leaned her head in the doorway and whispered, 'Just wear the short socks, Maree. Long ones are so daggy.' Having recently found a new word, she used it all the time.

Maree said, 'But I am a dag. Don't you know, I'm a sheep.' She stuck her tongue out and said, 'Baa.'

Her sister gave her a folded-arm look. There was no room in the bathroom for one sister and one dag. She left.

Maree rubbed water over her cow-licks and pressed them viciously flat, to no avail. Shrugging, she put on her long socks, with rubber bands under the turned-down tops to keep them up over her calves. They stayed up better that way when she played at being a horse.

FOUR

Their father was not insensitive to wishes in the house. If anything, perhaps he was too sensitive. He thought he heard echoes where there were none.

Once, passing Maree in the hall, he said, 'What did you say, smart-mouth?'

At other times he pre-empted desire. He came home with bags of goodies, sweets and nuts, or flowers in green cellophane and ribbon for their mother. Silently, Mrs Sterry would take the flowers and put them in a vase.

All forms of control require the impression of generosity.

One day he stepped into the lounge room, a man whose bulk could fill a doorway and draw shadows upon opposite walls. Maree and Lissa turned.

'What's say we get a dog, kids?' he said.

They gasped. Maree said, 'Dad, please!'

Lissa shrugged and went back to her magazine.

Their father sat in his customary chair and forgot about

it. He had perhaps had only given vent to a passing thought. But even the most casual of suggestions could inflame Maree's imagination.

As the wishful dreamer of the household, she began to read books about dogs. She read how to train a dog to sit, beg and stay. She began to pester her parents about when they might be able to bring one home.

When that failed to elicit a direct response, she worked upon Samantha to render the girl susceptible to doggy suggestions. It was up to Maree to close ranks. She wanted a dog of her own, therefore she had to involve her sisters, including Lissa, who did not particularly care for animals.

One day, when her father was sitting reading a newspaper, Maree said, 'Dad, what about the dog?'

Annoyed, he said, 'What dog?'

'You said we could get one from the pound.'

'When did I say that?'

'A little while ago.' Her mother came into the room and frowned at Maree. Beleaguering requests were bound to result in bad moods for all.

Her father said, 'Oh, I don't care. Go to the pound whenever you like, for Christ's sake. Let me read the paper.'

That afternoon, Maree said to Lissa, 'Dad said we can go to the pound whenever we like.'

Lissa was plaiting her hair into slender tails. She looked like Marcia Brady. Television was always creeping into their lives like that. Maree detested Marcia Brady, perhaps because her sister sometimes reminded her of her. She said, in a slightly whiny voice, 'Did you hear?'

Lissa, finishing a plait, shrugged. 'What do you want a dog for anyway, Ree?'

'For, I don't know, a *friend*. It could wait for me after school.'

'Don't you have friends already?'

Just then, Samantha came in with a kewpie doll on a bentwood stick. She waved it so that it flapped. 'Auntie Leslie gave me.'

They said, 'Shh.'

Auntie Leslie was an older woman who lived in a brown house that smelled of musty timber down the street. Because it was a brown house, or because it smelled of musty timber, or because she was a single older woman, it was widely perceived in the neighbourhood that the house would soon be replaced. She was nobody's auntie, as far as anyone could tell, and all her children had upped and left. They had left her as cuckoos leave a nest.

Maree's mother was constantly saying no to or thanking the woman for trinkets and ice-blocks handed over the front fence for her children. The kewpie doll had filtered through in a sort of direct, black-market deal between Sam and the woman. Running home, Samantha had fallen and grazed both knees. Because of her tears, she had been allowed to keep the doll.

Now she started pulling at the doll's bow. It was impossible to talk when she was in the room. For a start, she would cross and recross in front of her older sisters just to capture their attention. She so loved attention that it did not seem to perturb her if they grew angry. Lissa and Maree had a silent sentence, a sort of lip-read that went 'Such a brat!' followed by false attentiveness. They said, 'That's lovely, Sam.'

Maree, co-opting, said, 'Samantha wants a dog, don't you?'

'Doggy, doggy!' Samantha sang. Lissa frowned and picked her nails.

Maree was not prepared to give up. She said, 'Go outside now, Sam, and tell that to Mum. Go on. Go on. Because Dad promised we could get one.'

The girl flounced out again, dragging her doll. In a minute their mother was at the door, holding Sam by one arm, glaring at Maree. She said, 'Did you tell Sam we could get a dog?'

Lissa was sighing in irritation. Samantha looked confused; she hated, more than anything, to feel that she was missing out on something. Before Maree could answer, Samantha started to wail.

Maree's mother raised one eyebrow, an expression Maree secretly stored away for her own future use. She knew that she would have to practise to develop the right style. Unconsciously, she began testing her own forehead for the appropriate muscles.

Lissa said, 'Why don't you just get her one, Mum?'

Everybody looked at Maree. She was the culprit. 'Dad said we could,' she moaned, flinging herself on the bed.

Their mother let Samantha go and looked at all her daughters unevenly. She appeared to be about to say something. But a sudden defeat made her shoulders droop, and her eyebrow returned to its twin. 'I'll talk to your father,' she said as she left.

Lissa, still picking her nails, said, 'That's it, Maree. Always get what you want.'

Samantha danced around them in glee, as happy at being the cause of something good as she always was at being the cause of affront.

That evening, their father came into their bedroom just

before bed-time. Lissa was rubbing hand cream into her feet; Maree was lying on her bed reading.

Their father said, 'All right, a dog, is it? Who's going to feed the thing?'

Maree said, 'Me.'

'Teach it to sit?'

'Me.'

'Pick up dog crap when it shits?'

She looked at her father balefully. Lissa had her fingers to her nose and was saying, 'Phew.'

He said, 'All righty. A dog it is.' Then he sauntered off down the hall. Maree went to bed in a sort of lush content. She wanted the biggest dog available, a Great Dane. This was her chance to overcome fear. No boys would throw stones at a girl who was thus protected.

Before letting them go to the pound to find a dog, their father thought it necessary to instruct his daughters in the particularities of cost. He was the king giving his daughter a money purse for her to prove her ability to purchase wisely.

He said, 'That's what he'll cost. And then there's food. You think this money comes easy? You think it grows in my wallet, kids? Let me tell you, I work bloody hard for this money so I can pay to keep all you.' He was showing Maree how much the dog would cost.

Maree said impatiently, 'Yes Dad.'

Their mother was moving about the house looking for her handbag and continually interrupting, 'Is this the car key? Where do I put petrol in? How do I turn on the lights if it starts to rain?' Apart from once or twice having picked the children up from school, the last time resulting in the bus accident, their mother rarely drove.

Lissa was lying on the front verandah covered in

Jennifer Kremmer

coconut oil to try to work up a tan. She declined to come
along. 'Maree, it's your dog,' she said vaguely as they
passed.

They heard their father shout, 'Get in off that front
verandah—no daughter of mine is going to parade in front
of the world dressed like a, like a hussy!'

Lissa, face burning, scrambled back inside.

Mrs Sterry had to be instructed which way to drive to
the pound. She was a nervous driver and had to be told
again. As she drove, she said to Maree, 'I don't want you
treating it like it's yours. It's the family dog. It'll stay
outside. And I expect you to keep your end of the room a
bit tidier than you have in the past.'

She drove in small lurches, prone to sudden lags behind
traffic so that she always missed the lights. The rear-view
mirror seemed to bother her greatly and the steering wheel
sat too high. Always, the absent presence of the masculine
driver—the fact that she had to realign the seat, set the
mirror—made her wobbly and uncertain.

At the pound rows of dogs beseeched Maree and her
mother and sister to choose them. All ears rang. Surrounded by shit piles and with the desperation of the truly
doomed, dogs launched themselves at cage fronts, snarling
or yelping piteously. Eventually Samantha took her finger
out of her mouth long enough to clutch her mother's dress
hem and start crying.

Maree kept hopping from cage to cage, looking for the
one. The only. The dog. They all either pranced too much
or had iffy, stained hair.

Finally their mother pointed to a nervous, skinny cross-
breed with a short yellow coat and ribs like a xylophone.
The dog shivered against the bars. They'd already passed
him twice because of the mange on his rump.

'He'll be perfect,' she said confidently. 'He's already desexed, and the fur will come good.'

Maree scowled. This was just an ordinary dog, like any other dog, only mangy and unkempt. Then she put her hand in through the bars and the animal licked. She felt sorry for him at once and thought perhaps he would be okay after all. He seemed to accept her readily enough. She nodded gravely to her mother.

On the way to the car, walking the dog on a piece of old rope, Maree was chattering. 'We can call him Calypso, or Fauntleroy.'

Samantha squealed as the dog licked her arm.

Their mother shushed them until they got home. Suddenly quiet, nervously watching the dog in the back seat as he shivered against Maree, who was happy as long as she could pet him, she seemed to be second-thinking. Her face was strained.

Their father did not get out of his chair. He had put the newspaper aside, however, and the first thing he said when they led the dog into the house for his approval was, 'What the hell is that?'

Their mother's nervousness congealed. She said defensively, 'It's a dog, what do you think it is?'

Maree said, 'It's a bitser.' She'd thought it was a breed, the way her mother had said it.

Irritation made their father's face swell. He said, 'Why in the hell did you get such a runt? Look at it! That's not a dog, it's a bloody piece of string, it's a walking skeleton!'

Their mother took the dog out through the kitchen to the back door. Her face was bright red. Opening the door she said, 'What's wrong with him that a little bit of food won't fix?'

Their father said, 'Look at him. A runt.'

Mrs Sterry closed the back door and the dog sat on the back step, his skinny tail thumping. The girls watched their mother. They were not allowed to go outside. Consequently each thump sounded excrutiatingly pitiful. Even Lissa had come into the kitchen to see what was up.

'What's that noise?'

Mr Sterry said, 'Mind your business.'

Their mother did not look at any of her girls. While their father angrily picked up his boots and took them into the bedroom, Maree and Samantha stared about the room vaguely, without speaking. They had picked that dog because they had felt sorry for him. Now they felt sorry for themselves.

The next morning, their father took the car for some new tyres, so it was safe to play with the dog. Maree kept showing Lissa how to hold food out so that he would remain sitting until they wanted him to eat it.

'No, Lissa, like this!'

They were fighting over what they were going to call him. Maree said, 'Prince. Darien. I know: Champion.'

Lissa said, 'He looks like the pyjamas I used to have. Remember the yellow ones? And he's so soft. Hey there, Mr Pyjama.'

The dog licked her hand.

Maree said, 'Let's not call him Mr Pyjama. Mr Pyjama.' She said it with disgust. 'Mr Pyjama. That's so typical, Lissa. Mr Pyjama.'

'He likes it, look,' her sister continued. 'He's wagging his tail. Aren't you, Mr Pyjama? Mr Pyjama.'

Maree said, 'What about, I know, what about, um, um.' She couldn't think of a name. She was watching her sister and frowning.

Then she ran inside. 'Mum!' she called, 'Mum! Lissa wants to call him Mr Pyjama. Do we have to call him that?'

Her mother was lying on the settee with a facecloth over her eyes and one arm up behind her head. In the kitchen, morning radio met the smell of boiled eggs and cold toast. It was a Sunday like any Sunday. Her job in the house was never done.

Maree hated the dog from the instant her sister's name for him was accepted. It was accepted because Maree was overheard by her father saying to Lissa, 'If you keep calling him Mr Pyjama I'll burp in your face.' Her father, striding down the hall, put his angry head around the bedroom door.

'If I hear you mouthing things like that again,' he shouted, 'you'll get the hiding you'll never forget. All right?'

Maree whined, 'But Dad, Lissa wants to call him a stupid name like Mr Pyjama.' She did a little dance, sing-songing, 'Mr Pyjama, Mr Pyjama,' with her face in contortions.

Their father moved into the room and gave Maree a light smack on the cheek.

'All right, Miss?' he asked squarely. 'Now Mr Pyjama it is.'

Later, climbing around the swing set, Maree said, 'Stupid Mr Pyjama, stupid Mr Pyjama.'

It was as though, because their father was cruel, or because he looked at the dog they had bought and said, 'Why the hell did you get one so starving? The damn thing's half dead!' Maree became cruel. Every time the dog licked her hand, even though his tongue felt warm and friendly, she slapped the end of his nose. She felt herself to be above the dog. Not only that; because of the name, she felt herself above her sister.

Their mother was steely. Reprimanded, she ceased to be involved at all in the creature's well-being, and merely added to her shopping the requisite cheapest cans of dog food, which Mr Pyjama bolted and perpetually wanted more of. She stood on the back step, empty can in her hand, and looked at him with a look that might have been sympathy, or might have been disgust.

Maybe she was thinking of what it meant to have never had a pet of any kind, or of how her mother had once fed rat bait to the pigeons that flocked in their backyard from a neighbour's pigeon shed. Or maybe she regretted her part in bringing the animal to the house. Perhaps he was better off starving in the pound.

They owned the dog for three weeks. Every day of this period their father kicked it aside with his foot or said, 'There goes a useless mutt. What a waste of money.' There was always a fight over whose turn it was to fetch the dog's dish and whose turn it was to open the can. Later the fight changed to who had to feed him, because nobody wanted to go into the backyard. He jumped up on them too much and the yard was full of dog shit.

If their father, walking in the backyard to look for his toolbox, got dog shit on his heel, he would stand on the back step and yell at somebody to come and scrape it off. Disapproving of his family's choice of pet, he punished them for every turd. All through this, Mr Pyjama continued to pant and approve. He seemed to like every gesture, even those that might have seemed cruel. A ball thrown against the wall was no less indicative of good humour to him than one that pelted into his doggy ribcage and briefly stung.

The dog rescued them all by escaping one day when

the side gate was accidentally—or otherwise—left open. Nobody saw him leave; he was just gone.

Their father put his work boots on and marched down the street with his hands cupped about his mouth shouting, 'Here, dawg!' It was not in him to use the animal's name.

Maree lay on her bed and cried. She cried so much that she was astonished, looking into the mirror in the bathroom, at the depth of her grief. Her dismay over Mr Pyjama's loss was not at all in proportion to the degree she had valued the dog. Indeed, it was unrelated to any of the events of the preceding three weeks.

Every night, Maree pleaded with the ceiling above her bed for the dog to return. 'Dear God, dear God, please please please please please let Mr Pyjama come back. I promise promise promise promise promise I will not leave the gate open ever again and I promise promise promise promise promise I will never feed him potato peelings and I will remember to give him water, I promise promise promise, and I will believe in You, God, I promise.'

Since nobody brought the dog home and he never returned, there was obviously no God.

For three days she went to school with a tear-sodden face and laid her head on the desk in her arms, waiting with trepidation for the teacher to pick her out and be sympathetic, or accusatory.

She loved her teacher, though she thought him sometimes cruel.

In a way, she wanted him to be cruel. She wanted him to be more like her father. It was necessary for her to imagine cruelty in order to imagine kindness or love.

Then Danielle, her best friend at school, said, 'There was a dog on the side of the road this morning. I was looking out the window of the bus and there it was.'

Danielle lived near a racetrack. Their friendship was based around animal stories.

Maree shivered. 'Was he tan? Was he about this high? Did he look a bit skinny still?'

Danielle nodded.

'Oh, oh, was he still alive, was he breathing? Did you look, could you see?'

'No, I couldn't tell.' Seeing Maree's face, she added, 'Well, yes, I did see his eyes open, I think he was looking around.'

Their teacher strode into the room and failed to notice Maree or her tear-stained face. This was both a hurt and a balm to Maree. It was sufficient to rouse her from worrying over the dog to worrying about what her teacher thought of her, or if he thought of her. Lately he had been forgetting her name. Lately, too, she had been forgetting to think up lies for why she had not done her homework.

'Okay, class, who's got some answers for yesterday?' The teacher was as handsome as a statue.

Everybody reached for their books.

That afternoon after school, Maree told her mother that their pet was somewhere out on the road and had been seen by Danielle. 'Can we go and look for him? He might still be alive.'

'That girl, what's-her-name, is an out-and-out liar. Your father rang the pound this morning and they've got him, so how can he be by the side of the road at your bloody friend's bus stop?'

She looked so annoyed she seethed, almost the way their father did. But her seething was smoky. Her seething was wrapped in a shroud. Her cigarette came and went in her hand like a wand.

Maree said, in a way that was both irksome and reasonable, 'Can we pick him up from the pound, then?'

Her mother looked at Maree, and her head was slightly on the side. Smoke curled indecisively around her hair. She stubbed her cigarette out in a jam-jar lid and said, 'Ask your father, since he's Mr Generosity.'

Lissa was already beginning to forget they even had a pet. She spoke about Mr Pyjama in the past tense. 'Well, Maree, you never really liked him. Maybe it's better this way.'

What was wrong with her sister, Maree realised, was that she was innately happy. Whenever anything bad happened, she thought it was for the good. She thought everything led somewhere, like paths in a benign forest lined by nettles that occasionally pricked one's fingers with warnings to steer clear, stay on the right road.

When their father was due home, Maree waited, fuming, for the first tread of his heavy boot on the porch. She did not care about right roads. She wished to veer off the path, to storm the nettles in a fury and damage her hands. All roads, right or otherwise, led to her father. This was because he enabled things.

As he wiped his boots on the welcome mat, loosening each one with the other's steel-cap toe, Maree was haunting the doorway. Before he had even looked at her she said, in one gasp, 'Dad, Mum says they found Mr Pyjama. Can we get him back again?'

Her father was often kind. This was the distracting thing about him. It was as though he timed his responses to his children by some sort of inner clock of receptiveness or violence. He loved his children to the extent that he had to punish them for their inadequacies. But occasionally their inadequacies spoke to him of his own.

These were the moments when he was wholly unpredictable.

This evening, caught at the doorway, he said, 'We are not spending another cent on that idiot dog, and that's final.'

FIVE

By the time they were both in high school, Maree and Lissa had been made overly conscious of wastefulness. When young they always shared a bath. If one of them took the risk of topping up with hot water, she invariably got an angry command to turn it off. Sharing bathwater made them competitive. Sisterly affection was not a fixture of the house, it was a by-product. And it was subterranean.

Because sisterhood was unreliable, being a by-product, the sisters often fought over inconsequential things, such as setting the table or making coleslaw. Anything, in fact, which involved helping their mother with domestic chores.

Dinner was the coming together of whatever constituted and reinforced the family, the house, the suburb. Their mother cooked mashed potato, leek and bean stew, lamb chops and diced carrots. When the table was set, Lissa, Maree and Samantha would curl into lounges or pretend to do homework or play with dolls on the floor until their mother called, 'Is anybody going to eat?'

Jennifer Kremmer

Their father would sit at one end of the table, while their mother moved to and fro from the kitchen to fetch pepper, salt, butter, butter knives, dishcloth, saucepans. The television always made the lounge room seem more appealing than the dining oom. There were cries for somebody's chair to be moved out of the way. Even though they were sitting at the table, the whole family's heads craned to see what was on in the other room.

They heard explosions, gunshots, nasal twang. That other room was always capturing their attention, hostaging their thoughts. This was the ulterior purpose of television.

In a lull, Samantha asked, 'What's this?' of the meal on her plate. Having just started pre-school, she was fussy and prone to moods.

Their mother said tiredly, 'It's a wigwam for a goose's bridal. Eat it up.'

The little girl hated to be teased and slapped her spoon into the meal. 'It looks yucky,' she whined.

Their father said mildly, 'Well, kiddo, it's on the table, so you're not moving until you eat.'

A strange aspect of parents was their ability to point at something unlikeable and say, as sternly as a commandant, 'Eat.' Around food, conversation was not pursued. Maree's father merely pointed to a morsel and said, 'Food. Eat.' This was his economy of words.

Samantha howled, but all eyes were temporarily downcast, or searching for something out of view. Losing her sense of connection, Samantha turned to her mother. 'I don't want to, Mummy, I don't want to.' When she cried, her face looked like a rubber mask pulled in separate ways. It reddened and paled simultaneously, turning into a fright of a face, a haunted face. Maree suspected it was the face she wore herself when she cried, and this self-knowledge made her cruel.

She said, 'Shut up, sook.'

Lissa said, 'Leave her alone, Maree.' She had a soft heart and was always sticking up for the wounded. Apart from being a beauty, she wanted to be a nurse.

The patriarch turned upon his girls. It was not in him to allow any other forms of authority. 'Lissa, Maree,' he said, 'do keep your face shut.' The word 'face', as he used it, had an ulterior reference that was often dire. He often called Maree face-ache, usually in jest. It made her feel her face was out of line.

For Samantha, he turned the dial of his reasonableness up a notch. 'Children in India have nothing at all, kid,' he informed. 'You eat, or you'll get in trouble.' It was easy to see that behind reasonableness lurked justice. Justice, in all its punitiveness, was the saviour. When things got out of hand, it would step in front of reasonableness like a policeman in front of a crowd.

Their mother just kept getting up to move things or to place hot dishes on the coasters or cold dishes out of the way. She barely looked at anybody. Her children were not her children, or if they were she did not love them. Or she loved them, but she was as subject to the policeman as a bystander.

In the end, Samantha whined a fraction too inquisitively, 'But Daddy, *why* do I have to eat?' At this point, everybody looked to Mr Sterry to see what he would do. He was no more happy that they had looked at him than he had been to hear his daughter's whine. He perceived a tendency to altercation, suspected a plot to overthrow his order. Instinctively, he began to feel in his back pocket for his wallet.

43

Justice shoved reasonableness aside with a stern hand, and their father slammed his fist down onto the tablecloth. Plates jittered and clanged. Leek and beans spilled in grey-green gobs. The policeman could arrest, handcuff, shoot or ignore.

Leaning across the table, their father divided the food on Samantha's plate into portions. He concocted a simple rule: 'You have until seven o'clock to eat this bit.' He was pointing for her benefit to the cuckooless clock in the next room. 'See that? That says five minutes to seven. Do you know what that means?'

Samantha gazed at him slackly. Drool slipped stringily to her chin.

'It means that you have five minutes to eat this much. If you haven't eaten this bit here by the time that big hand moves onto that twelve, you're going to get a smack.'

The older sisters continued to eat mechanically, without enjoyment. Maree briefly imagined, safe for the moment, that when she was Samantha's age, she had never caused this sort of trouble. In the kitchen, their mother ran hot water into the sink.

The clock ticked.

Samantha sniffled babyishly. She mashed food up with her spoon but it would not go anywhere near her mouth. Of the three girls, she was the most prone to blatant misdemeanour. Therefore it was most important that she be taught the meaning of rules, even the simplest, such as the necessity to be docile in regards to what the patriarch provided for her. What his labours had earned the funds for the bringing home of. She must eat.

Maree and Lissa had already undergone these lessons. In Maree the knowledge made her reticent, but some sisterly feeling caused Lissa to put down her own fork and say, 'Dad, does she have to eat what she doesn't want to? Can't she just—'

Their father opened his mouth to roar, 'Did I ask for your comment, smart-mouth?' It was as though this outburst were precisely what he had been waiting for, and, now that it had occurred, the actions of Samantha in eating or non-eating became somewhat incidental. As though he were testing, in fact, for insurrection.

Lissa left the room in a fluster of near-adult indignation.

The house rules were paranoid rules because other forms of family constituted a threat to the established order—this was his rule. Sisters must not conspire to thwart the rule. When they sought independence, the girls were brought into line. But when they conspired, they were punished.

As a result of these procedures the girls often tiptoed around, in case they were incriminated. They took care to seem aloof.

On any particular morning, Maree would get out of bed, creeping past the soft snoring of her older sister, to go to the toilet. If there was somebody in the bathroom, she would listen for her father's throat-clearing behind the door. She could not stand there waiting because at any second he might open the door and say, 'What the hell are you doing? Were you spying on me?'

Or he might be in a good mood and say, 'Sorry, kid, the mirror's fogged.'

When Maree was small, her father would sometimes lift her up just below the armpits, causing her crown to bump against the ceiling. Googly-eyed and teary, she always pretended it did not hurt, but since then she lived in fear of the plaster above.

Standing outside the bathroom door, Maree listened for

some sign that her father had had, or was about to have, his shower.

Her mother walked past in loafer slippers and with an absent look. Passing Maree, she said, 'Eh?' as though Maree had said something.

Maree pretended to look in the cupboard for a towel. Then she went back into her room and lay on her bed. Lissa, lying on her own bed, cocked one eye and said, 'What's up with you today, face-ache?'

'Shut your face, loober lips.'

Lissa never seemed to feel insults, and her own were always given in a sort of jest. Mostly she did not insult. She'd say, sitting up and stretching, 'Oh, Maree, isn't it a lovely morning!'

Maree just shrugged.

At the end of the hall the toilet flushed. Their mother put her head inside the bedroom and said, 'Are either of you two girls getting up today? It's quarter to eight!' Neglected by the household's system, their mother always fought for it. It was one of the peculiarities of her lot.

Most mornings, Samantha would be up already and playing with her dolls, avoiding having to look at either of her sisters, for she might see what was in store for her when she was their age. For their part, the older girls usually ignored her. Lissa sometimes gave in to a belief in an instinct to mother the child; she helped her don shoes and occasionally tucked her in and read to her of an evening, while their mother was ironing. But in the mornings, the older girls had an external focus. They looked pityingly or annoyedly at their youngest sister, or even snatched favourite toys out of her grip just to bring on her steady wail, specifically in order to then thwart the wail by the reward of the very same toy.

Lissa was just re-entering a gangly phase. At thirteen she had suddenly shot up and at sixteen she was developing a sort of lanky womanliness that threatened to become a perpetual allure. The transition from bralessness to the wearing of a bra had not seemed to cause Lissa any undue anxiety; rather the reverse. She was permanently cheerful in ways that often irked her younger sister. When boob-tubes were in fashion, Maree wore a boob-tube. It made her breasts look like swollen jellybeans.

Maree was in an awkward phase of being both gangly and somewhat squat. Because she was the second sister, second to Lissa, everything she did was comparative. She could feel the awkwardness in her own body and the effect on her ability to flee at a sudden onslaught; she often felt trapped or at risk. Oddly, she was most comfortable in the shadow of her father, where at least her anxieties had a locus.

Elsewhere, nothing could be predicted.

Her older sister made late-night confessions of a sexual nature to Maree. It was as though it were Lissa's duty to narrate the possibilities of Maree's first contacts with the opposite species.

For example, a hairdresser once put his hand down Lissa's shirt and told her she was 'too firm', she needed 'a good massage to make her breasts soft'.

Maree said, 'How rude.'

Lissa, telling this to Maree well past their bedtime, a disembodied voice in darkness, said, 'Oh, no, Maree, he was pretty nice about it.' She had thought the man's hand had felt surprisingly soft, like a girl's.

Lissa was just old enough to want to go out and to come home later than she was officially permitted to, and to lie about why that was. Their parents could not have known what she really got up to. Their father must not, or he would have seen to it that she never went anywhere without a chaperone.

Lissa had kissed boys deeply, drinking bourbon from their lips. She had almost been fingered while wearing a tampon.

When describing it, she did not use the word 'finger'. She said, 'But then his hand went down there and I said no.'

Both Lissa and Maree would have blanched at the term 'to finger'. It was boys' talk. They shared a rare respect for how terrible boys were, at least in language, at least the boys around here.

Even vinyl boys were a part of Lissa's gangly repertoire; she bought singles by unnameable bands with spare change from lunch money saved up over weeks, relegating them to a dusty pile under her bed. A miniature record player made of pink and green plastic was the household's only music appliance, a cast-off from a vacating neighbour. Their father, in an access of generosity, had fixed the belt.

The record player annoyed Maree. Tizzy sounds emanating from the closed bedroom door were sufficient to send her careening around the house with her hands over her ears, promising to move out when she was old enough. But she would never behave like this when her father was in the house. Her threats were confined to the afterspace between school and his homecoming. Thus they were empty threats.

Their mother ignored Maree when she performed. Sewing at the dining-room table, curtains making voluminous piles to one side, she would concentrate all her being into feeding fabric toward the needleplate, as though sewing were a saving grace.

The windows acquired checkered frills and ruffles; the venetians tasselled cords.

One afternoon, Lissa flounced into the bedroom. She studied Maree, who was reading a horse book, and eventually said, 'Why do you insist on wearing long socks, Maree? They're so daggy.'

Maree looked up from her book. Incensed, she said, 'When are you going to grow out of Estace the Pestace?' Leaping off the bed, she began to swivel her hips low to the ground and form her face into a spasmy croon. This was in reference to Lissa's professed love for Elvis Presley. The girl had been so in love with him that one day a year or so ago she had burst into the bedroom crying—what had happened was that the heart-throb had died. Maree had said, 'Oh, who cares? He was dead in the head anyway. Estace the Pestace, a real dead-head.'

But Lissa was not really scratching for a scuffle. She just wanted to get Maree's attention, and had been affronted to find her sister so engrossed in a silly book. There were undercurrents she needed to stir.

So she ignored Maree's Elvis comment and sat in front of the dressing-table mirror and began to preen annoyingly. It was clear she had something in her bag that she was pretending she did not want Maree to see.

Therefore Maree began to pretend that she did not want to see it, and got back on her bed to continue her book. But her forehead was creased and her fingers locked as she inwardly fumed. Every movement of her sister drove Maree into a fury and she would swing on Lissa with a vicious 'Stop it!' The waiting game belied some powerful drives.

Eventually Lissa sighed and began sliding her birthday bracelets and bangles up and down her arm to maximise

Jennifer Kremmer

Maree's inability to concentrate. She said, 'Hey, Maree Curie, can you keep a secret?'

Maree folded down the corner of her page and gazed across the room in irritation. She said, 'Yeah, Lissa Listerine.'

Her sister sat up straight, forgetting the bangles. Her face became cloudy with guile and even a trace of fear. She made a great demonstration of going to check the hallway and closing the door. Then she came right up to Maree's face and whispered, 'It's the biggest secret ever, Maree, and if you ever tell anyone I'll be kicked out of home.'

Maree said, 'So what?' Her sister drew back, so she added, 'All right. What is it?'

Lissa pulled a package out of her bag covered in blue and white chemist logos. She said, 'Guess.'

Maree, squinting, knew what was in the packet and what it meant. At the same time she saw the destruction of the family, which could not survive such a brazen affront. She tried to unremember the secret, but it was there, solid in her gut. A time bomb. The Pill.

What was inevitable was that Lissa would be found out.

Lissa said, 'I got them today. Boy, what I had to do to get them. The doctor was a real jerk.' She tittered nervously. 'He said he hoped my mother approved of what I was going to do.'

'What a jerk,' Maree agreed.

She watched as her sister unpopped a little pill from the pack, listened briefly for footsteps, and slipped it into her mouth. Lissa hid the rest of the pills among her underpants in the top drawer.

Maree, watching her sister hide them, knew without knowing that in that drawer lay disaster just a mother's wash-and-fold away. But she did not say so to Lissa, because part of the knowing of the secret and the non-relaying of it was also, in a strange way, holding back on its repercussions.

Still, Maree considered that to look at Lissa, anybody would probably think, There goes a girl who is on the Pill.

In the aftermath of this moment of confession, Lissa acted nonchalant and Maree listened for the call to help in the kitchen. When it came, they refused to look at each other. They opened the bedroom door and went out to appear dutiful or reassuring. The plaster did not crack from the walls; the house remained standing.

Their mother rarely looked up when they came into a room. Or if she did, it was as though they were invisible and she could only trace their whereabouts through noise or impressions upon floorboards. She had just finished hanging the new curtains over the kitchen window and had started peeling potatoes for dinner.

She said, 'Where's Sam? Oh, there. Well, somebody give me a hand.'

Lissa always jumped to her mother's aid. She did things for her that nobody, including her mother, saw as doing things; they were just things that were done because somebody had to do them.

For the moment, their mother moved through them all as though they were her ghosts. Once or twice she actually did seem to notice Lissa, as though the girl's demeanour made her suspicious, but since Lissa had become so good at hiding things, nothing was said.

Their father came home and wiped his boots on the mat. He looked at everybody, at something in their faces that suggested the complicity he always feared, and said, 'What's up?'

51

Samantha showed him her doll. She said, 'Daddy, her arm came off.'

He grunted and moved her aside. Only after he had removed all traces of his tiresome day, placing his wallet and keys atop his bathroom shelf, reassembling himself in the family way, did he arrive back in the situation to reassess.

He was a man sensitive to complications and effects. He had an ear for danger signs. He was a man who desired to remain fair. Fairness would mean everything would be all right in the end. He was a man who wanted everything to be all right. This was his secret, his fear.

He wanted his daughters to love him.

Through dinner, the girls were silent. Their mother moved to and fro with plates and food.

After dinner, they spread themselves across the lounge room. Maree was colouring in. Her mother stood in a corner of the room folding washing. Every now and then, her eyes slid to the television and away.

'How about somebody gets your mother a cup of tea, eh?' said their father.

Lissa and Maree exchanged a glance of wilful dare. Lissa was almost always the one to make tea, but now she shook her head at Maree. She defaulted; she was tired, or had a headache or a secret hangover.

Maree made the tea for once, in a sort of dread.

She stood fretfully near the kettle, watching it boil. She poured hot water into the teapot, waited, and poured the tea into cups. She took her father's tea out first, intending to follow the rules regarding the order of serving: father first; everybody else second. And do not spill. Frightened of spilling, she could only take one at a time.

Her father appeared to think she had made him tea

instead of making it for her mother. He waved her across the room, saying, 'No, your mother, give it to your mother! Make her a cup, I said.'

Mrs Sterry, who had been staring through the television into her own reflection for the duration of the tea-making exercise, shuddered momentarily at having been asked to participate. She said, as though the tea in the cup Maree held was poisonous or of an unknown quality, 'No, I don't want any. Give it to your father.'

Her father said, 'What's that, love, you don't want a cuppa?'

'No, no, I don't want one, I had one earlier.'

The conversation might have ended there, but did not. Maree's father interpreted his wife's note of distress as something that needed cajoling into humour. In a good mood himself, he was unable to allow the bad moods of others.

Being the one who set directions, things were simple for him: up, down. If he stood on his head, he would wonder what was wrong with all the upside down people in the room. He would keep on about it until they really thought they were upside down, or until they went to their rooms to practise standing on their heads.

So when Maree's mother refused the tea, he frowned and said, 'What's up, love, don't you feel well? Not even a cup of tea your daughter's freshly made for you with her own hands?'

Mrs Sterry hurled a towel onto a tipping pile and said sharply, 'I said no, I already had a cup and I do not want another one. Can't you see I've got stuff here to do?'

Maree was blushing at the phrase 'own hands'. She looked at the cup of tea in her fingers and felt them burning against the china. She stood in the centre of the lounge room, in the way of the television, with the cup in her hands, wondering what to do with it or what to say. A horse could rise up out of the carpet just then, and vanish her from this lounge room in a blink, leaving her family gaping at the hole in the floor.

Her father, exasperated, said, 'Well, bring it here, then.'

Maree and Lissa looked idly, almost in disbelief, at one another, then looked back to the TV. As they turned away, their mother returned to what she was doing. There was no expression at all upon her face.

Sometimes the lounge room was a difficult place to be.

At some point in an evening, such as when a particular image appeared on the TV and caused their father to clear his throat and cross his legs, it was time for the children to go to bed. The cuckooless cuckoo clock chimed the hour. Even Lissa, at sixteen, would be glanced at curiously if she stayed up past ten.

Lissa often did so, but this necessitated enduring the knowing glances of her mother and father, who both took it upon themselves to say, 'You know you have to be at school tomorrow.' Ever fearful of a regression to their own education, in sheds and orphanages, they plied their daughters with reminders to do well.

Maree, on being asked to go to bed, often felt guilty about not having looked into her textbooks. She would make small, uncertain incursions into her homework and leave the bulk of it undone. In the nuclear family, the only study was inward; knowledge only had a place if it came from the centre. And, of course, it was not really study. Most school knowledge failed this simple test and therefore could not be used in the home. School knowledge was like a gadget bought in another country where sockets or electricity were differently contrived. It was meant to make life easier, but seldom did.

Putting her books back in her schoolbag, Maree often went to the kitchen and got herself a glass of milk. This was considered to be raiding the fridge. Halfway through her milk once, she called out to the lounge room, 'Mum, can I have a glass of milk?' She couldn't have said why she did this. Perhaps she felt guilty.

Her mother called back urgently, 'Yes, oh, well, no, don't have milk, there'll be none left for your father's cereal! Have water.'

Maree stared at the half-glass of milk and shook the milk carton. It was about a fifth full. Finally she drank one more good gulp from the glass and poured the rest back.

She slunk from the kitchen, looking out for spies. Samantha had not yet gone to bed. Playing on the floor with a doll, she looked up at Maree and said, 'Um-ah, you had some milk. I saw you.'

Maree said, 'I did not, dobber.'

The little girl stood up in her yellow floral pyjamas and went into the lounge room singing, 'Mu-um, Maree had some mi-ilk!'

Maree's mother made some small noise of annoyance. Maree froze like a rabbit in headlights until sufficient time had elapsed for her to feel safe enough to continue on her way.

But even in her bedroom, Maree could not be safe. The walls of her and Lissa's bedroom were flimsy gyprock, the door hollow plywood. They lived in a time and space not their own.

Danger was a part of the family structure. It surrounded each girl in a force-field through which the other girls rarely passed, for to make known their link outside the jurisdiction of the father was to render it obscene. Force-fielded, hemmed in by wants, Maree was doomed.

Danger was there in the walls, the rafters, the bedrooms and the connecting hall. It followed them into rooms and ate off their plates. It was in the concept of family itself, for whatever is nuclear may decay.

SIX

Long before the time in which the dog was merely an interlude, Maree had begun alleviating claustrophobia or carsickness by imagining a horse running alongside the family car when they went on long drives. Its hooves went da-doom, da-doom, da-doom.

At traffic lights the animal pranced, dodging old women with shopping trolleys and men in singlets. It leaped off kerbs onto roadways, veered out of the way of oncoming cars, and formed imaginary lines on the window-pane.

Despite the horse, when Maree was much younger she often got carsick. Stopping the car, peering into the rear-view mirror, Maree's father would say, 'Uh-oh, old face-ache's sick again, is she?' He would ease the car onto a shoulder while everybody looked out a different window Maree would hunch, glowering, in distress.

Being in the family made her wish to be sick.

All their limbs brushed, Maree's and her sisters', and

the rigidity of her father behind the steering wheel was almost comic. The back of his head held a coin-sized bald spot. Nobody was game to mention it.

Sitting in the car was worse than being in the lounge room, more hemmed in.

Leaning out of a held-open door onto roadside gravel, Maree would imagine the clip-clop of horses' hooves as the animal waited invisibly while she retched. She reassured herself by her ability to retain her connection to her imagined horse while being sick.

Spittle made pathetic white beads against the steely gravel. In the background, traffic swished past and beeped or cheered. Her mother would swivel in her seat to wipe Maree's face with a hanky as she lurched back into the car.

Lissa, leaning away as far as possible, would remark, 'Phew, there she goes again, Dad, old spew-guts Maree.' But as Maree returned to her seat Lissa would pat her arm or offer her a tissue to wipe her face.

The drive would resume where it had left off, a few dozen cars behind in the traffic queue.

Later, Maree began to draw pictures of horses. She began at about the age of ten, and never stopped. Now she drew constantly, in the margins of books, on the covers of magazines, on spare paper. Occasionally she turned a horse into a dog, or vice versa.

Sometimes, putting down her pencil for a moment, she would ask, 'Mum, do you think I could ever have a horse of my own?'

'Where are you going to put it, love?'

'I don't mean here. What about if I'm older?'

'If you're older, dear, you'll have other things to think about.'

Her mother was sometimes in good moods like this,

not because of anything anybody had done for her, just because the cloud of her mood had spontaneously lifted, usually while their father was at work. She would look at the drawings Maree presented for her perusal and say, 'That bit there needs to be a bit wider,' or, 'Mmmm.'

A slightly less positive 'Mmmm' than usual could send Maree into paper-ripping spasms of tears.

The way Maree drew had a pattern to it that seemed so fundamental that in later life she would absently begin telephone doodles or stick figures with the same central curve. She always started a horse at the point where the hind leg meets the flank, thus:

Then:

Then:

59

And finally:

She drew her horses with points all around the edges, like spikes. Curved, yet spiky. They looked right to her. Sometimes she pressed the point of a hock or hoof right through the page.

She sent these drawings to the weekend newspapers, but none ever appeared in print. The two-dollar prizes were won by girls with names like Shelley Newington from suburbs that sounded like their names. Shelley Newington probably had her own stable full of horses. By contrast, Maree's suburb and the surrounding ones were all called Something-estate or heights, and the newer ones mews or grange.

Perhaps Maree never won a prize because she was never happy with her drawings, and always tried to fix them up after she'd traced over the pencil with indelible ink by cutting around the shape of the horse and sticking it onto clean paper, or sending it in as it was, a floppy cut-out thing that she had to fold the legs of so that it would fit into an envelope. Or maybe it was because her drawings were on butcher's paper instead of white cartridge paper with embossing. Newspapers never wrote back to say they had got her drawings; the things simply disappeared without trace.

Maree often did four or five drawings at one sitting. But she posted them separately, until her mother, in a vague irritation, said, 'I do not have the money to keep spending on stamps.'

So Maree took to sending a few in a single envelope every couple of weeks. She always ran to get the Sunday paper and be first to turn to the comics page in order to see if a drawing of hers had been chosen for publication.

Maree thought, because this was what school and everybody told her, that if a person kept trying hard to be the best at something, eventually their efforts would be rewarded. School was awash with such fallacies. It was as though the teachers nostalgically swept the students with the same brushes they had been painted with. Having never met the mythical place in which it was possible for their own talents to shine, they contented themselves with brandishing the remotest of possibilities before the students. They called it merit. Nobody ever told Maree to give up, to just be mediocre.

They could have saved her a lot of ink.

To inspire people with the desire to outperform those who had come before, the teachers lent her the idea that she was an individual: only individuals could reach excellence.

Maree, individual, ambitious, eager to please, reflected upon her lack of success with the horse drawings. It seemed to her now that there was no such thing as success, there were only pre-set paths.

Maree, drawing horses, was doomed.

The field in which it was possible for her to excel seemed directly proportional to the space between her and other people. Looking at her parents as though they were not her real parents gave Maree the sense that she belonged to the world, that she could excel in it, and be rewarded. She began to search her family for signs that she was not at all like them. She borrowed speech patterns from neighbouring kids that set her apart. She developed tics and ruses. Standing in front of her mother, rattling off a narrative of her day, for instance, she would unconsciously adopt the hands-on-hip pose of a friend from school, and punctuate each sentence with a careless little 'huh'.

She found proof of her being unlike the rest of her family in that only she wished to own a horse, only she liked to draw. Neither of her parents showed either inclination. Lissa, tall and gangly, with long hair that the perm was always falling out of, sat about on weekends watching pop music on television, or listening to the stereo with headphones on, only looking up when her father, in dramatic irritation, bellowed across the room, 'Would you shut that bloody thing off when your mother calls?'

Samantha, baby-pudgy, unformed, was somehow acutely aware of what would cause her sisters anguish. She once drew in indelible texta tears on the face of Maree's favourite plastic miniature horse, and she had a habit of tapping on hard surfaces with bits of timber or stray twigs, causing Maree or Lissa to yell, 'Cut it out!' This would merely make Samantha giggle. Or she would relocate her entire bedding to the lounge room to make cubby houses and then sit inside the mess pretending she was invisible when Maree passed through.

The family was full of incidents that proved it was not Maree's family.

Maree's father spent his weekends watching sport or falling asleep in the recliner rocker with his mouth open, head back, one of his arms dangling near a forgotten teacup. This was his basic home pastime, the way he recovered whatever living a life outside the house took out of him.

Maree decided that she was an orphan or abductee who was living with this family only until the people who had put her there returned. In this manner she had been able to get through the onset of adolescence.

Because she imagined that she was only temporarily living with her present family, other people who had some relation of power to her and who were benevolent about it, such as some of her teachers, became potential real-parents.

In primary school there had been Mr Bixby. He was their only teacher in sixth class; a singular hero. Later Maree's crushes became diffuse. It was hard to have crushes upon teachers who only taught for an hour at a time. Maree, imagining that she was secretly related to Mr Bixby, stopped answering to anybody around the home. Her mother would slam cookery into the oven with tea-towels, shrieking for Maree to set the table or wash some spoons. Maree would hide on her bed with her hands over her ears. Her mother became tired of hauling Maree to her feet or slapping the outside of her thigh.

Her parents had just thought she was being difficult. Nobody could understand her, and even Lissa had stopped trying to please her for the effort it took. Her mother wore a 'told you so' air. Her father would come home from work and say, 'Where's face-ache today?' He said this in Maree's earshot, with undertones of fondness.

Maree imagined scenarios in which she ran away, some-times to Mr Bixby's house where she was kept as a surrogate daughter until she grew old enough to leave. Imagining that Mr Bixby was her father did not merely affect Maree around the house. She held her breath when-ever he stood behind her to glance over her schoolwork.

She wanted to ask him, 'When am I coming home?'

She once hated Danielle's mother for daring to comment, after picking them up from school, 'That teacher's a handsome young man, eh?'

Danielle had said, 'You better ask Maree, she's in love with him, aren't you Maree?'

Maree had said, 'Am not!'

Maree hated anybody who looked at her teacher without respecting the fact that he was related to her.

One day, Maree overheard a conversation as she ran on an errand past the staff room. She slowed to a protracted dawdle.

A teacher was saying, 'And of course Phil doesn't care if all the schoolgirls in the place have a crush on him, and not just that what's-her-name, the Sterry kid.'

Another teacher laughed and said, 'Look, who wouldn't?'

It shocked Maree that she had been capable of giving away her thoughts, and to people she knew only at a distance. And it shocked her that they, teachers in a school, had their own desires for each other.

The world seemed suddenly astonishingly complex.

Mr Bixby decided to draw each of his students' silhouettes one day, and they had to each sit on a chair in the hard light of an overhead projector while he traced around their shadows in pencil. His pale, man's hand held the stick of graphite without trembling, smoothly drawing the outlines of the children.

But Maree, last to be silhouetted, quivered so much with the fear of proximity that her teacher lost his temper. 'Keep still, or you won't get yours done!' It was the first time he had ever been angry at her, and it reminded her of the way her father, tired after his day's labours, often misheard a comment, and thought he was being mocked.

She had been so scared of making her teacher angry that she had made him angry. Mr Bixby began to pack up the overhead projector while Maree, with her sad, untraceable outline and a pair of scissors, began to cut out the shape of her face.

Maree realised that men, fathers or not, were in some manner all the same.

She saw that the outline of her profile looked so different from the outlines of every other pupil that her face must have been malformed. Yet by day, when she glanced into the bedroom or bathroom mirror, she saw that she was not distinctive: there was nothing about her face that was unusual. Her features were mobile in the way that other faces were mobile. She laughed or glowered or smiled. The expressions of her face were similar to those of other people.

Yet she knew she was different. What marked her out was something secret; something familial.

While Mr Bixby's back was turned, she carefully trimmed her outline to try to lessen its differences. She made the nose smaller. She increased the distance from chin to throat.

When she passed it to Mr Bixby, who was standing on a chair with an impatient hand out as he hung all the profiles on the wall, hers was an outline that resembled his.

Maree was embarrassed. She could not watch the handsome Mr Bixby tacking it to the wall with a drawing pin. She stood about the base of his chair and her face became red with a new and unsharable knowledge.

She suddenly did not want to be his daughter. She did not want to be anybody's daughter. She wanted to be a horse, and gallop hard across a salty plain somewhere with wind blowing in her mane and nobody able to catch her.

Mr Bixby said as he climbed down, 'It's not a great likeness there, Sterry. You just couldn't keep still, could you?'

When Maree quit primary school for high school, she took with her a habit of staring out of the classroom window whenever the teacher spoke. She could not forgive teachers for being ultimately like her father, or for being able to say of her when she walked past the staff-room, 'There goes a girl who has a crush'.

While looking out the window, Maree imagined her horse. This kept her from having to imagine school.

Gazing out of a classroom window, she would see the horse walking along the grassy verge. Occasionally her maths teacher, growing impatient, would interrupt this amble with a bit of thrown chalk. On these occasions he would say, 'You'll never become a vet if you don't learn algorithms.'

Maree resented being brought out of her imagination. She would stop looking out of the window and cast her eyes down so that the teacher could not see the daydream in her expression. When the teacher had turned back to the blackboard, she would gaze out of the windowpane again. Sometimes she was distracted by the graffiti on the desk; 'Jane is a big sloppy slut', that's what one desk said. It made Maree feel hot, as though her middle name were Jane, as though she were a sloppy slut. Or as though the teacher had been able to read her thoughts and knew the exact reason why she was imagining a horse, even when she did not.

On the way home from school, Maree would shiver behind the glass pane of the bus, while Lissa would sit at the back next to her best friend Andrea. Together they would pass notes to boys and twitter like birds granted a forest of sweet fruit.

Because of Lissa, boys left Maree alone.

She borrowed and read library books about horses, and her best friend Danielle shared her passion. Danielle was always telling Maree about this and that horse and this and that jockey. Maree was not interested in the jockeys, but she hung on her friend's every word about horses. Together they ignored school. They spent periods out of class poring over stud books, guessing at the bloodlines of the horse they would one day have. Teachers meandering past in the yard would click their tongues at Maree and Danielle.

Most afternoons, Maree sat on her bed and drew horses. She knew the outlines of horses and every point on their bodies. She knew how to draw them jumping, or galloping away from packs of wild dogs, which snarled and snapped from her pencils, breaking the lead.

She learned to ride from books, from stories of girls who learned to ride, and wished she did not have to wait until she was an adult to have a horse of her own. Still, Danielle and Maree had a routine that went:

'Dad says we might be able to have a horse next year, if we're good.'

'My mum says if I save up every bit of lunch money . . .'

'I saw a horse go down my street yesterday and it had a loose shoe.'

'One day I'm going to buy a thoroughbred.'

'Mum says my next birthday present is going to be lessons.'

Danielle did eventually have lessons. Envious, Maree placed a pillow over the piping fence and practised upon that, with shoelaces for reins, her calves dangling in empty space.

Her mother stood on the porch with her hands on her hips and shrieked, 'Is that one of my pillowslips you're getting covered with dirt? Get it off and bring it inside this minute!'

Of course it was her mother's pillowslip: Maree owned nothing. Her mother owned all the sheets and bedding. She owned the pots, pans and plates and the vacuum cleaner and the washing machine. Her father owned the rooms and the walls, the timber and brick and the ceramic tiles in the bathroom, the concrete paths and the eaves. He owned the rooftop tiles and the ceilings. He owned the floors and the way his kids sat on the floors. He owned the television aerial.

Removed from the fence, Maree headed for the bedroom, pillow and slip dragging on the concrete path, face set in a scowl the mirror of her mother's. She had no way to ask for a real horse apart from the droop of her posture. She wanted to be seen as a child who suffered, whose only wish could never occur.

It was there, in Maree's hidden and shabby interior, that the secret percolated. She desperately wanted her parents to see that she was suffering, to rescue her with the one purchase.

When Maree was thirteen, ponies came clopping into her street. Squealing, she ran outside to stand by the crumbling letterbox with her heart in her mouth and stars in her eyes.

She kept wishing, Oh, give me, give me. She wanted the . . . the white one, no, the black one. She waved at the riders. She willed them to stop.

The riders waved back but kept going, as casual as princesses visiting a lesser part of the realm.

Maree did not go inside again until long after the

animals had disappeared down the street. She could not bear the thought of being alive without a horse of her own. She wished for one so hard that when each birthday or Christmas brought her only a new book or toy, she made sure her thanks could not be mistaken for heartfelt.

As a consequence, she was simply thought to be unpleasable. She stopped eating what her mother served, or toyed with food on her plate. Foolishly dramatic though these gestures were, they had effect. Maree's parents began to look at her sideways, out of the corners of their eyes.

Her father became obsessed with pleasing her simply because she was never pleased. He brought home chocolate bars, holding them out to Maree and her sisters and watching to see which one she chose. Maree, seeing the trick in this, would say, 'I don't like any of those chocolate bars, but thanks anyway.'

Watching her sisters eat the squares, Maree's mouth would water. It was as though, only wanting one thing, she would rather condemn herself to having nothing.

Her mother never bothered to try to please Maree, she merely watched Maree from the edges of the lounge room. Perhaps something about her daughter frightened her, being so like something in herself.

Next door to the Sterry house was a piece of land that had once been set aside for a new main road. Some years before, the roadway plan was cancelled and the vacant block was divided in two and sold to the two houses either side. The Sterry household had somehow managed to remortgage itself for the purchase of the half-block, and suddenly the family had an extra fifth of an acre, a paddock about the size of an ordinary backyard in which Maree's mother, in the first spring, grew ears of corn, to the derision of the children on the school bus, and in which over the ensuing months neighbourhood dogs shat and cats coupled and poisonous spiders spun webs. Gradually this small paddock filled to the neighbour's bricked property line with old garden implements, a broken washing machine, disintegrated garbage bags bursting with unused bathroom tiles, odd housebricks for a contemplated addition, strips of aluminium siding, and galvanised tin sheets.

As though to certify something about her family, Maree would climb through the loose palings that shut this paddock off from the backyard and sit amid her family's detritus.

When she learned that Danielle was to receive riding lessons, Maree went to sit in this paddock and put her forehead into her hands and imagined that she, Maree, was a horse and would never have to go into the house again.

She did not want to *ride* a horse. She wanted to *become* one.

SEVEN

Danielle told Maree one day, 'Mum said it's okay if you come riding with us'. Maree's stomach fluttered. She spent the afternoon in a tizz, waiting for her father to come home.

He walked in, cheerful enough, and Maree made both her parents a cup of tea. Their eyes flitted from her to one another and back.

Lissa, sitting on the lounge nearest the television, said, 'Maree's sucking up for something, aren't you Maree?'

Her father said, 'Do you mind?' He disliked schoolyard talk, and found the term 'sucking' crude.

Maree said, 'Mum, Dad, can I go horseriding on Sunday?'

There was a blank pause, then their father cleared his throat. 'What do you propose to go horseriding on?'

'There's a riding ranch about half an hour away. Danielle and her mother will go too.'

Her mother seemed to assume that this would not be allowed. As though to give her husband justification, to reinforce his rule, she said, 'Have you tidied your room at all in the last month, Maree?'

But her intervention caused Maree's father's sense of fairness to rise. Appraising first Maree, then his cup of tea, he said, 'I guess it can't do any harm, can it darl?'

Her mother gaped.

Maree ran and gave her father an awkward hug. Lissa choked back a sarcastic 'Ugh.' The things Lissa wanted were all easy things, like cheap records and the odd tank-top. She could save up and buy them herself.

Back in their bedroom, she said, 'Just like you, Maree. Always get what you want.' There was an element of envy in her voice.

When the horseriding day arrived, Maree changed three times into jeans, tracksuit pants and then jeans again. She wanted to look like a rider. All she had for her feet were sneakers.

Her mother, standing in the bedroom doorway, said, 'You can't wear sandshoes. If the horse treads on your foot you'll lose your toes.'

'What then?' Maree asked miserably. Her anticipation turned to abjection.

Her mother pointed under the bed. Maree's school shoes were the only sturdy ones she had. She looked at the school shoes, groaned, and looked away.

Lissa, lying on her bed, said, 'They'll make her look stupid, Mum.' Lissa understood the importance of not appearing daggy.

Maree finally shrugged. She put on the black shiny shoes, in deference to her toes. She even started singing as she tied the laces up.

Danielle's mother drove a white Cortina, which she parked somewhat askew. She was a large woman with

slicked-back hair and a shirt with silver flowers embroi-
dered on the chest. She had decided not to come into the
house but wait in the car, which slightly appalled Maree's
mother.

'Oh, hello,' Mrs Sterry said, in a voice with a scratched
tone.

Danielle and Maree crept into the back seat and played
punchings. Danielle was wearing a black velvet riding cap
with a piece of leather that sat right on her chin. Her legs
were clad in wondrous elastic cloth that she brushed aside
with, 'Oh, these old jodhpurs.' They had double-sewn leg
insets. And she wore riding boots, leather with elastic sides.

Maree, wearing school shoes and jeans, was doomed.

When they got to the riding ranch an hour later, a light
rain was falling. Danielle's mother was anxious and kept
gazing up at the sky, her neck so broad it made her head
appear tubular.

'I don't know if this is going to work, my girl,' she sang
to Danielle.

The way she said 'my girl' had a fond ring to it. It was
clear she was worried for her daughter. She seemed to
think nothing of having to wait in the car for her daughter
and daughter's friend. Perhaps, like a wild and famished
stoat, Mrs Bywater was the sort of mother who did not
mind self-sacrifice.

Danielle was dismissive. 'Mum, you worry too much,'
she chided, slapping her riding crop against her thigh. She
peered at the sky, where grey clouds hovered, and briefly
flattened her palm. As though in sympathy the splatter-rain
stopped.

'Oh, you, you,' Danielle's mother laughed, and waved
them on. She steered Maree and Danielle into a stable
where a woman with a clipboard was jotting down names

and pointing people toward a queue of horses. The horse smell assailed Maree first, all clod and earth and green mulch. Horses shuffled or rested their great hooves, looking boredly about. They were all saddled or waiting to be saddled. People in the queue ahead checked watches, giggled, looked concerned or yawned.

Maree kept staring at the horses. They ranged in size and shape from small white ponies that barely came up to her waist to lanky, bone-backed animals that had probably once pulled a plough. Their weight upon the hard-packed earth was ponderous. Every now and then, a hoof shaking off a fly thudded into the ground and Maree inadvertently jumped.

She had to fill in a form. Danielle's mother looked over her shoulder with good grace. Under the question 'Have you ridden before?' Maree wrote 'yes'.

Danielle's mother said, 'Is that true?'

Danielle was looking away. Maree supposed that she would get a better horse if she pretended to be experienced. And, she thought, having read so much, she would surely know how to ride and would not need help. She did not want a horse that merely walked everywhere.

So she nodded and Danielle's mother pretended to believe her.

The queue shuffled forward and the sun came out. Excited girls paled and quietened when their mount was led to them, some having to be helped into the stirrups while others shrugged off assistance and plonked themselves astride. Wafts of moist horse shit filled the air. The hoofbeats as people rode away were terrific, like in a cowboy movie.

Danielle kept nudging Maree's arm and saying, 'I hope

I don't get that one. He's got splints,' or, 'Missy Smartypants up there can't even hold the reins.'

Danielle was mounted first. Her horse was a rumpy black creature with tufts of long hair along the backs of his lower legs and a Roman nose. He snorted equably at his rider and sent his nostrils on a broad arc to snuff at her riding boot. Equally good-naturedly, she pulled him around.

It was Maree's turn. A vast bony dun was led in front of her by a thickset young man with a new sprout of beard who looked at her without curiosity. He had blue, slightly anaemic-looking eyes and dark eyebrows. Gulping, she made for the saddle as she had seen her friend do, but the man's tongue clicked and he said, 'Hard hat first, sport.' He pointed to a trestle table behind her.

Bashful because she'd forgotten, she found one that fitted. Then she fumbled the stirrup as she placed her foot inside the metal cup. Maree always stumbled when it was most crucial to appear competent. Blushing, she tried again, but again her foot slipped out and she hopped briefly, not knowing which part of the saddle to hold.

The man sighed through his nose. He handed the reins to the woman with the clipboard and came around behind her. She found herself suddenly hoisted up and landing in the saddle with an agitated thump. Air seemed to condense around her face. Danielle gave a spurious cheer.

A man two horses ahead of them was having trouble turning his horse from the mounting shed and was attempting, by sheer force, to swing the animal's head out to the pastures. His arms stuck out at right angles to his body, making a sort of bow and arrow of the horse's neck.

Maree, thinking that the man was steering correctly, stuck her own arms out perpendicular to her body, and at the same time, knowing this was the thing to do, gave her horse two small kicks in the ribs. The saddle, creaking ominously, lurched and the horse, with Maree roughly in the seat, moved off after Danielle's.

Suddenly the world was too far away. Everything was in motion, including Maree's own heart. But the horse knew its routine and was ambling along without, it appeared, a thought in its head. It knew the way to go.

When Maree caught up to her friend, out of breath from fear and sure that she was going to fall, Danielle leaned across and said, 'Don't pull the reins like that, do it like this.'

She showed Maree how to keep her elbows in. Every now and then, Maree's mount sensed her incompetence and jerked his jaws down to snatch at grass. For the rest of the ride, it was all she could do to keep his muzzle bobbing at the correct neck's length away, more or less steering ahead, while keeping her hat from slithering down over her eyes.

They cantered once, for a stretch of about ten metres down a dip and up again, in between trees. Maree saw Danielle flying ahead, her horse's solid backside and hind hooves pummelling the dirt, and then her own horse followed suit and she was flying, in the air and out of the saddle and then down again, hard hat falling onto her eyes, wind whipping her hair about her face, and so exhilarated she could only go, 'Whoop! Whoop!'

At the end of the canter, Danielle reined in and they spent the rest of the ride at a bumpy trot. Coming under the stableyard boom once again, Maree felt like a warrior returning from battle. Her horse had settled into his bony strides without much fuss.

When she described the ride to her father afterward,

she raved about how they had 'galloped', unconsciously dramatising so that he and the rest of the family would know how confidently she had kept herself and her horse under control.

Her father said, 'Hmmm—galloped, eh?' and went back to reading his paper.

EIGHT

Once upon a time, according to history books, the horse was a motor car. It was a machine to be built, fitted, raced, tinkered with and compared.

To Maree, it seemed that no masculine use of an object was too far-fetched. It was history.

No wonder Maree only liked English and Art. They were the only subjects with spaces to hide. Hiding, she daydreamed constantly of being a horse.

As a horse, she imagined she galloped along beside the family car, witnessing in glimpses the slack unconsciousness that was the family. Lissa, momentarily sulking with her lower lip protruding because the radio station was not tuned to pop music; Samantha, shaking her Barbie doll at the back of their mother's head; their father, on a perpetual lookout for rules to enforce; their mother, her lips pursed, staring ahead.

Every now and then, Maree's imagined horse was forced to jump a fence or leave the family car to gallop down a culvert when the side of the road dipped. Sometimes these separations forced her to be Maree in the car, again steadfastly gazing out the window. She was bored to be herself again. The glass freeze-framed her as she waited for the culvert to disappear, and when Lissa, on a pinching mission, squeezed her elbow in an attempt to wake her up, Maree shoved her elbow quickly into her sister.

'Oh, snotty,' Lissa murmured. But Lissa was incapable of sulking for long, even about pop music or her sister's bad moods. In a minute her head was nodding to a song she had remembered from the morning's radio. The buzz of pop made her absolutely happy.

In Maree's imagination, the horse reappeared at the other end of the culvert, racing now against steel rails, over an overpass, behind a bus. She didn't always have to be the horse, just so long as she could see him galloping.

Always, when the drive was over, Maree imagined that the horse went to sleep somewhere dry, in pale straw. She even fed him before she went to bed at night. She had an array of simple rules for her own fantasies, such as that if she took her mind off the horse for too long, he would grow skinny and perhaps starve. Therefore she had to constantly be alert. If she forgot him for too long, her invented horse might disappear. So she set to imagining him in a fancy stable, surrounded by grooms. She drew pictures of the stable as well as the horse, though her pictures never quite looked the way she wanted them to.

The stable contained so many extra rooms it was like a palace. There was even a grand arena, which Maree had drawn in plan, and in which she sometimes imagined riding or being her horse in front of vast applauding crowds. She danced, pirouetted, bowed and jumped obstacles.

Each night when she went to bed, she launched into a sort of long story, exactly like a dream, except that she was directing it. Meanwhile, the house creaked around her; her sister snored. The light under the door winked out and footsteps took the last of the family down the hall to bed.

To begin with Maree would watch slabs of white light stream around the ceiling. Lissa breathed deeply and sometimes moved slightly, as though she slept in small fits. Through the half-open venetians that they had forgotten to close, Maree could see the stars. While she was awake, the stars actually travelled across the sky.

In her imagination, she was alone in the family back-yard. At this stage of the 'dream', she was still Maree the girl. She was standing in the backyard in the middle of the day and it was raining and the reason she was a girl standing in the rain was that her father had sent her out of the house for fighting with Samantha.

So she was watching the back door for some sign that her father was about to step outside and tell her she could come back in. She was waiting for him to be sorry, or for her mother to come to the door with a dry towel to rub her hair, the way she did when the girls came in from sport.

Instead, Maree could hear in the house her mother shrieking at her father and the slamming of cupboard doors. She heard the certitude in the voice of her father as he steeled each word so that nothing her mother said could have any effect.

Maree looked down and saw that instead of hands she now had solid blocks like pieces of heavy wood. She moved them together experimentally and they made a clopping noise, familiar from cowboy movies. When she was little, she had loved anything that resembled a clopping noise and often tried to make that noise with her hands or tongue.

She clopped her hands together like a horse. The blocks at the end of her arms were hooves. And then, instead of arms she had forelegs. Putting her hooves onto the back-yard earth, she left hoofprints.

Becoming a horse, everything elongated: forearm turned into upper foreleg; elbow moved back toward ribcage, which developed in height; neck crunchingly extended itself so that the head was as mobile as a jack-in-the-box; and the whole body, horizontal now on its stilted front legs, became rounded and long, like a cylinder.

Her feet lost their toes and her heels lengthened, sharp-ened and became hocks. Her rump aired a tail to the afternoon wind and her neck shook its sallow mane. When she laughed, it was the sound of a horse's whinny. Flexing her neck, she saw knees and fetlocks. Her head could swing great arcs on her supple neck. She looked to either side and to the rear and saw the smooth points of both hips, her burnished flanks. She captured the sky in massive degrees, the clouds sweeping each arc of vision, no longer full of rain but white and fluffy.

Her school dress lay trampled in the dirt. In the house, the television absorbed the silence between her mother, her father, Samantha and Lissa.

Maree whinnied and the venetian blinds of the house flickered. Her father opened the back door to deposit a bulging plastic bag in the garbage bin; the lid clanged. Her mother appeared and disappeared from the kitchen window as she moved between television and kitchen, parting the curtains every so often to see whatever it was she saw when she looked out. Maree might have said something to her mother, but her new voice was a neigh.

Between a high-pitched whinny and a voiceless neigh, she was without speech.

She lunged her new horse-shape at the palings between the house and the side yard, then backed up and leapt right over it. The wind was so sharp that it stung her nostrils.

As a horse, she had left suburbia. She was surrounded by bush. Whooshes of air moved in and out of her rounded nostrils. She listened to the air as though it could tell her where to go. It was a sound she had never heard as a girl: herself breathing, living.

She might have been galloping for hours or days.

She trotted along a hillside down to a patch of trees. Between the trees there was a sandy stream. Maree found a clearing beneath the trees and rolled in the sand. Then she stepped into a slow, flat section of the stream, which came up to her knees, and rolled again so that all the dust and foam and sweat were washed away. As she dipped and rolled, old drink containers, drinking straws, bits of plastic and paper floated down the stream and away.

In Maree's reverie it was late afternoon. She cropped a little of the spidery grass that sprouted between trees and rocks. She was in a valley of small hillsides not yet marked for development, an oasis in the suburbs. Or perhaps it was really the edge of a great wildness where bears might roam, except that there were no bears here.

There were possums and echidnas. A flash of light and chortling announced the path of a parrot. She drank from the stream and watched lazy horsehair worms and water snails drift along in the shadow of her face; she was startled by her own eye, which blinked its fringe of lashes back at her. Minnow-carp darted in the shallows and tiny potato-nippers rose to the surface, took air and dived again. Eels stirred muddy eddies. Broken beer bottles glinted, lost to human mouths.

Maree lifted her muzzle from the water and let a cascade trickle from her chin. Her eyes caught every motion, although the world through her horse's eyes was black and white. She could differentiate the underside tremble of a clover leaf at the waltz of a beetle from the top-blown shiver of the wind. She could tell the slow whorl of water as a tortoise moved below from the coil of ripples around a submerged stick. Pampas grass from bullrush; skeleton weed from scotch thistle. She could see ant legs as ants climbed the bark of ash trees before rain.

At this point of the waking dream, Maree was always tense, expectant, knowing that she was about to lose track of her imagination and fall asleep. She wished she could keep imagining, but she could not. Ordinary dreams took over and twisted what she wanted. At times, they were nightmares.

Sometimes she woke very early and lay in bed listening. The grey light that encircled the room made her sister's sleeping form a region of hills, and the pallor of the window a faraway sea. Then she was happiest of all.

Waking, Maree was inevitably a girl. She would be exhausted. As a girl, she was always here and there, shrinking, stumbling, falling apart. She had no real control over anything she did. She got up, went to breakfast, polished her shoes. She squeezed past Lissa to get to the toothpaste tube, she apologised when she was supposed to. But these were the programs of a robot.

She hid her cereal bowl so that she could throw the cereal away when nobody was watching, after taking a couple of mouthfuls. She half-believed, since it suited her imagination, that she could transform her body, which was why she often let herself go hungry, and why hunger felt like its own justification. Maree could go whole days without eating what her mother dished up, even though she got sent to her room or shouted at or, sometimes, begged. It was her favourite thing to be sent to her room because it meant she was no longer surrounded by the temptation of food and could go into reverie as she pleased. And she didn't have to wash up. She could hear them doing it, in the kitchen, her mother and Lissa.

But hunger was hard to deny. She sometimes sneaked out at night while they were all watching television, and pinched sustenance from the refrigerator.

At school, Danielle and Maree compared how much they consumed over the course of a day. They compiled lists of food as well as lists of what they would need to buy if they ever owned a horse. Maree drew pictures for her friend in class and Danielle sent them back with comments like 'a bit long in the legs' or 'can I have a long mane on this one?' In some classes they were made to sit at separate desks.

Danielle's parents were different to Maree's. They lived on a bigger block, though Maree's had a side yard. Danielle had already had twelve riding lessons; Maree had only been for one ride. When Danielle asked for something, they said, 'Well, if you promise to make your bed.' They never defaulted when their daughter failed her end of the bargain. When Maree asked for something, her father would usually say, 'Kids in India are starving.'

Maree could not pay attention in history class, or keep up with anybody else in sport. Running or jumping or diving off a local swimming-pool block, Maree always came last. The teachers looked at her and shrugged. They'd given up expecting anything more.

At school carnivals, when she was meant to be cheering, she found a book and sat somewhere. At lunchtimes she sat with Danielle and they picked through their home-made sandwiches then dropped them in the bins, or rationed themselves half a yoghurt each from the school canteen. Or they intoned to each other, 'I just can't eat anything today. I'm not even hungry any more.'

Maree would show her latest horse book from the library, and Danielle reciprocated.

After school Maree would see Lissa at the bus stop, where she stood with her long tanned legs catching looks from the boys. Danielle was always picked up from school in her mother's car. Maree was afraid of the bus stop. She was afraid of boys.

She would wait until the bus was about to pull up, put her head down and move towards it. She hid herself on the bus, in whatever seat she could find, and immediately resumed reading her books.

When she got home from school, Maree was always hungry. This was the most difficult time to deny food, because there were no adult strictures upon the eating of it. Generally, it was expected that the girls would raid the fridge in the afternoons, as long as they only took what was necessary for a snack. Maree would ensure that her mother was well and truly out of view before she glanced into the fridge's interior, and whenever she took out a piece of cheese or an apple she scurried with it into her room before beginning to eat.

She could not help a surge of glee when, staring into the bathroom mirror to locate an emerging spot, she noticed a dark shadow under the line of her jaw.

Because she only ate in private, otherwise resorting to subterfuges such as pushing the food around or complaining

of nausea, her parents thought Maree never ate at all. They
were convinced she was suffering a new teenage disease.
Consequently, they began to offer her more food at the
table, and to nudge each other as they passed behind her
back.

At the height of this surreptitious war, Maree felt rather
than heard herself to be the subject of parental conversa-
tions late at night, or indeed whenever she left the room.
Once, sitting upright on the floor in front of the telvision
watching a special on bowerbirds, Maree suddenly felt the
pressure of a foot in the small of her back. Her father said,
'You are getting far too skinny, miss.' He was so angry his
voice shook.

She could not turn to look at him because he would
have seen how much she smiled. Not eating was pleasure.
It was the only pleasure she could manipulate publicly.
She could not have found a more powerful form of dis-
obedience.

It was as though the less she ate, the stronger her
internal 'I' became. If she couldn't be a horse, then most
of all she would have loved to have been an invalid,
watching the world from her sickbed, like Velvet in the
film. She would have no need for a body at all.

She dreamed of being lighter than air. Of floating over
the school oval, above boys' heads. But whatever she
dreamed and however she starved herself, Maree always
woke up to real life. This meant shoe polish, school bag,
fending off buttered toast or cornflakes.

One morning, her father, polishing his own shoes, said,
'Are you going to eat breakfast, miss?'

'I don't want any.'

Her mother came into the room carrying a checkered
dress to iron for Samantha. Her eyebrows were lifted at

their facial extremes as though taped to the sides of her head; they looked like a devil's eyes. She glared at Maree. 'Is that girl not hungry again?'

It was true that Maree did not want to eat, but it was not due to lack of hunger. She whined, 'I feel sick. In the stomach. I don't want any food.'

Lissa came out of the kitchen, having finished breakfast, and breezed past Maree, unconcerned.

Maree headed for her bedroom. Her mother sang out, 'Come back here, miss, and eat.'

Her father said over her departing back, 'If I hear that you are not eating your lunch at school, miss, I'm going to belt you black and blue.'

There was nothing that made him angrier than this sort of loss of control. He provided; the family were meant to be grateful. Maree's father never forgot what he was angry about. Every black mark was in permanent ink. When she had showed him a bad report card once, he had said, 'So the smarty of the family is not to be, eh?' The coldness in his voice had made her ashamed. Now, even when she made an effort and did well in a test, he acted uninterested.

Maree could not describe her life to her father; she hated the world and everything in it. She hated report cards. The only thing she was good at was feigning lack of interest in food.

One day, when Maree had been very small, the Queen had been driven through the suburb along a cracked concrete highway. The school had given the children the afternoon in which to line along the roadside and wave, and when the black cars came into view, nobody waved more fiercely than Maree. Wanting to be noticed, she leaned out of the vague body of children and shook her little school flag. She wanted desperately to stand out.

But the black cars had passed with their windows tightly shut, and it had been impossible to tell which of them, if any, contained the Queen. The cars continued along the highway and were gone. The school children packed up and were ushered across the road on their way home.

Maree was doomed to want what she could not have. However, this ambition was not something special about her. It was the suburbs.

Pegasus

NINE

On the last day of school, Maree's mother was standing in the middle of the side yard in her pink washing-up gloves, gazing ahead of her, when Maree stepped off the bus. She had a look on her face that surpassed description, it just was. It was the same look she always had. This was Maree's mother going over and over the impossibilities of her life.

Maree walked toward the front door and trod on a slug. Black innards oozed along her heel. Disgusted, she took her shoe off and rubbed it on the lawn. Her life, as a girl in a family, was merciless, without end. All she wanted was to no longer be part of the family.

She went into the house and slung her school bag onto her bed and her shoes into a corner. Lissa was at Andrea's place, probably talking about boys. Only Samantha was in the house, and when Maree looked at her, the girl said, 'Well? What are you staring at?' Then she started to jig to and fro on her hips, poking her tongue out. Samantha's goal in the family was to antagonise others, or to occasionally expend upon them her vast capacity for glee. Each extreme was equally irksome. Maree slapped her.

Samantha ran outside squealing.

After a moment, their mother came in and her rubber gloves squeaked as they came off inside out. She had a way of putting them up to her lips and blowing them right again so that she looked as though she had a hand growing out of her face.

She glared at Maree. 'What did you hit Samantha for?' Samantha was her special pet.

'I didn't.' They both knew she was lying, so she added, 'Anyway, she deserved it.'

'I know who deserves a smack around here.' Her mother began flicking at flies with a rubber glove. Samantha kept peeking around her skirt like a fat rabbit. With a child's perfect timing, she stuck her head forward to pull a face, and just at that moment she was within reach.

Maree lunged. Her mother screamed, 'Don't you dare!' and whipped her with the rubber glove, which stung.

Rubbing her arm, Maree flounced up the hall to the bedroom. She shouted, 'I hate Samantha and I hate this house!'

'Well, stay in your room, then!'

Maree slammed her door. There was silence, and she had a sudden vision of her father, having decided to come home from work early, sauntering toward her with his shirt sleeves rolled.

The vision dissipated and Maree was alone in her room.

She emptied her school bag on the floor, enjoying the sense of mess as she saw the term's scrunched papers, lolly wrappers, hairclips, combs, fluff and unreturned textbooks cascade out. Sometimes Maree packed clothes or tinned food into her school bag and pretended she was running away, but she always slept through the nights of these planned escapes and in the mornings, chagrined, she unpacked and redistributed whatever she'd stowed. Today she kicked all the evidence of school underneath her bed, out of sight, and stuffed the bag full of casual clothes, knowing full well that she had no possibility of going anywhere at all. It was impossible to go anywhere. Maree did not even have a regular bus timetable. She owned nothing of importance, kept nothing, organised nothing of importance.

She was a girl in a room in a house.

She was still sitting on her bed staring at the wall when Lissa came in and said, 'What are you pooey about?'

This was one of their mother's terms—pooey—and Maree, rankled, said, 'Oh, piss off.' She said it quietly, afraid of being heard outside the bedroom.

In here anything could be said, provided it was said quietly.

Her sister sighed patiently. 'Well, if you don't want to tell me.' There was a long sneaking pause, then Maree sensed a presence on the floor near her bed and glanced across just in time to see Lissa crawling across the floor toward her, fingers curled into pretend talons. It was a game they used to play when they were little after the lights had gone out. Lissa had never really grown out of it. She was making faces and going, 'Ooooh, Mareeee.'

The door opened and their mother stood in the doorway with a dustpan and broom and something of a bemused expression. 'Get off the floor, Lissa,' she said. 'And both of you come and set the table.' She did not look at Maree.

Lissa, always ready to help around the house, jumped

up and dusted her hands. Maree sulked for a moment and then, simply to escape the bedroom for a while, decided to help too.

When their father got home he unbooted himself at the door, leaving his socks in a coil like furry snails. He took off his shirt and threw it onto a pile in the laundry and went about the house on bare feet, a reminder to his family of what he might have been like as a boy. He often reminded his family of a prior time. Seeing a silver car parked at the kerb of a shopping centre, he might say, 'Look at that car, kids. That's when they really knew how to make a machine that would last.' It was as though he were the only person in the world to have gone through eras of any significance.

Often, on arriving home, he ignored everybody and strode purposefully toward his bedroom, to reappear slightly paunchy and hunched, in thongs and singlet. He had been in the army reserve once, and he still liked to perform inspections. But his hovering was nothing compared to that of their mother. She constantly looked over people's shoulders. If he looked into the freezer, she would sneak up behind as though he'd peeked into the secret spot at the back of her bedroom drawer and found her menstrual pads. She would say, 'What are you looking for? There's nothing in there. It's a freezer, what are you hoping to find? Why don't you grab an apple, there's plenty of apples.'

Their father probably could not have said why he had to look in the freezer, the section of the refrigerator least likely to change, but for some reason he had to rummage through the Tupperware leftovers of dinners and packets of frozen peas, the latter used often as cold compresses when anyone had a headache. This evening, hearing the scrape of his wife's shoes on the back doormat, he shut the freezer quickly and turned away. Foiled, she gave him a hard look and disappeared up the hall waving a tea-towel.

With a tube of processed cheese in one hand and chewing noisily, jaw clicking, Mr Sterry surveyed the living spaces of his home. The table was set. He went to check that his daughters had finished their homework.

Maree was in the lounge room reaching for 'H' in the encylopaedia just as her father appeared in the doorway. She never did her homework, at least not until it was absolutely necessary. She paused, looked at him, and something conveyed in her attitude told him what she was doing, causing him to say, 'Uh-uh, Maree. Homework first.'

Gulping, she put the book back and made a sulky show of emptying books onto the floor from her school bag. Her father grunted and moved toward his chair. Samantha, sitting on the floor by the television and gluing glitter onto a fairy, said, 'Daddy!' She climbed to her feet and staggered toward him.

He said, 'Oof!' as she barrelled into him, and then swung her up into the air. Held above, her face reddened in pleasure and she lifted her arms over her head and said, 'Daddy, look, I'm a fairy-witch.' While Maree stared at the sums in the textbook that had been set as homework, Samantha gooed to their father. Lissa, having finished homework, was filing her nails.

Their father sat himself in his recliner rocker and, with Samantha attached like a limpet to his knee, jogged her up and down. He looked inordinately pleased; some obscure symbiosis kept the father-and-daughter routine alive long after Lissa and Maree had grown out of it. Perhaps this was the reason he had had children: this tireless little game. His knee was the hinge of the universe, the crux of a child's fun.

Jogging her, he was saying, 'One, two, upsie-whoo!' When she grew too heavy for his shin, he said, 'Okay now. Enough.'

Samantha reluctantly let him go.

The aroma of stew filled the lounge room. In the void between pretending to do her homework and being permitted to leave her books alone, Maree was imagining the ways in which she might refuse to eat her evening meal. She was imagining this, but her stomach was growling.

Their father was not really watching the television yet, so with a glance at him Lissa flicked the channel. He was a man who needed news or current affairs in order to relate to the world and his lounge room. But now, having tired of the game with Samantha, he was looking out of the window. Maree began to flip over and over the same page of her homework. She was waiting for him to focus on something else so that she might close her book altogether, but instead he began to squeak his chair back and forth on the heel of his thong.

Her father's gaze was outside, through the lounge-room venetians, where a neighbour across the road had finished watering his lawn and was uncoupling a hose. Maree's mother flitted in and out of view between hallway and kitchen. Cupboard doors began slamming in a laborious fashion. It was time for one of them to come and help carry what she had cooked onto the table. But nobody moved. There was a lull in the television programming and the screen turned black in the fraction after advertisements, then Maree's father cleared his throat. Samantha had demurely sat down and was contemplating her fairy.

The cuckoo clock did its hourly creak of ratchets, but no cuckoo appeared. Maree's father sat up and ceased his rocking. He said to the walls and television and not, seemingly, to anybody else, 'What do you reckon, should we get old face-ache a horse, eh?'

The rest of the room said, 'Wha?' In the family, it often happened that a favour to one of them resulted in a net loss in the well-being of the others. Samantha looked horrified. Lissa, clipping her toenails prior to polishing, let one fly across the room.

Maree whispered, 'Really? A real horse?' For a moment she thought he meant a picture of one; it would be just like her father to make such a joke. But her mother came to stand in the hallway, giving up chasing flies with her can of spray for long enough to listen.

'Your mother and I had a word about that side yard. It needs something to keep the grass down.' He was not explicitly looking at Maree, so she could not quite tell whether it was herself being addressed. There was something in the air that she could not pinpoint; a wisp of something that, in being proffered, also threatened. But she could not say what the threat was. Maree remained on the lounge-room floor, watching her father's face for the moment of doom, equally aware of her mother on the periphery.

She said suspiciously, 'A horse of my own?'

He nodded in a way that might have been sarcastic. Maree knew there was more; in a minute he delivered the crucial point.

'What I'm saying, daughter,' he said, as though he were talking to a brick wall, 'is that if you can start treating your mother with respect, and if you can get off this teenage starvation kick, we've decided we'll get you a horse.'

Lissa was gazing at Maree with her eyebrows raised. It was suddenly clear that Maree was meant to be jumping for joy.

Jennifer Kremmer

'A horse! A horse!' she shouted, and leaped to her feet, scattering her homework and textbooks.

Lissa wore a 'we know you're faking' look, and went back to her toenails. Her mother was still standing in the hallway with a can of Mortein, staring at the air about her for errant flies. She looked distractedly into the lounge room. It was impossible to know what she thought or felt, except perhaps about flies.

Her father said, 'Darl, anything to add?'

Maree's mother kept swatting the air about her head. 'You mean that she could be a bit more helpful around the house? And stop back-chatting me when I ask her to do something?' She paused and depressed the spray-can trigger for a half-second while she thought, aiming somewhere toward the cornice. She could stand a full ten minutes just listening for the buzz of outlaws. No method of domestic extermination was too toxic. She would hound a fly all the way around the house, spraying into rooms and closing doors, and even spraying over half-eaten cereal bowls and their childish heads. Windowpanes in every room were fogged in little circles where insects had met chemistry.

Maree felt the draining of some long-held and impossible fantasy. In becoming real, the fantasy had to lose something; shape, perhaps. What was meant by a horse? What manner of horse? Her father might have in mind a few riding lessons in a nearby estate, or a borrowed animal for weekends. Or the horse he bought for her might be so old that when she went to saddle it up, it would lie down and the RSPCA would have to be called to come and put it out of its misery.

Maree realised that her father was gazing at the ceiling in a frown. In a burst of intuition, she saw that she had not completed the appropriate formalities. So she said,

'I promise to eat anything I'm given. And I promise not to back-chat Mum, and I promise to help around the house without having to be asked.' Then she lurched to her father's chair and almost overbalanced it with the grandiosity of her hug.

Whenever the Sterry family kissed, a good-night kiss, for instance, or when their father suddenly piped up from the depths of his recliner rocker to say, 'How about a kiss from one of me daughters, eh?' it was on the side of the cheek, carefully, avoiding eye contact. Of course, had anybody said they were an undemonstrative family, he would have snorted, 'What the hell do you mean? We love our kids!'

Maree sidled toward her mother, who appeared to prepare herself for the worst. She said, 'Mind my burst blood vessel. Don't tread on that bit of the carpet, it's been sprayed. Oh, watch it, watch it, you're crushing my jacaranda seeds.' She had placed a fistful of the papery-fine seeds from a neigbour's windblown tree into her apron pocket and was anxiously turning away as Maree's arms snaked around her; but for once she seemed to melt a little at the warmth of her daughters response, and when Maree stood back from her she thought she glimpsed traces of moisture at the corners of her mother's eyes. This was so unexpected she gasped.

Samantha, watching from the floor, said, 'Daddy, can I have one too?'

TEN

If Maree expected anything at all, it was certainly not that her father would act quickly. But when she woke next morning she found him in the kitchen reading a newspaper. Her throat tightened when she saw he was circling classifieds. He looked up and said, 'Well, kidsies, who's coming for a country drive?'

Lissa said, 'Where to?' her curiosity linked to a deep suspicion of anything far away from boys or music. Their mother was wiping her rubber-gloved hands on a towel near the sink and her expression was mottled. Maree had just finished wiping up.

Her father said, loudspeaking across the room to his wife, 'What do you say, darl, want to come and look at a mule for old Maree?'

Maree squealed in an agony of delight so phoney-sounding, because she was not used to venting such an emotion, that Lissa made a sicking noise and scraped her chair back to leave the room. Samantha sat looking from face to face, as though in their faces might be read her future.

Their mother blew into her rubber gloves. Stowing them in the sink cupboard, she said, 'Well, as long as she's only going to look. That side yard needs plenty of cleaning up before she can put an animal in there.' This was the usual manner in which she spoke around Maree, in the third person, and looking through a window at the backyard or street.

Her father cleared his throat and jiggled keys and coins in his shorts pocket. He said in the direction of the kitchen window, 'There's no reason why we shouldn't buy her a horse today if we see the right one, darl. I've made a promise and I'll keep my end of the bargain as long as she keeps hers.' But for their mother's sake he added, 'Of course, Maree already knows she's not going to be the face-ache she used to be. She knows she'll get her homework done and clean up her side of the room. I only wish I could have realised earlier that all it took was buying her a bloody horse. I would have bought a stableful.'

Maree's mother said, looking directly at him, 'Not if you want this family to eat.'

Mr Sterry cleared his throat. 'Darl,' he went on, less loudly, 'if I want to pack a week's wages in a suitcase and chuck it off the Harbour Bridge, I'll do it. We'll eat styrofoam if we have to, as long as these bloody kids are happy.'

Their mother's face deepened in its hue like a sudden cloud, and their father tipped his teacup out in the sink and put his hands on each of her shoulders. She took a tissue and blew her nose into his awkward hug.

Samantha and Maree looked at each other, realised both their mouths were slackly open, and smirked.

Red-faced from the unnaturally public embrace, their

mother said, 'I just don't want her to get too excited in case we don't find what she wants. She has to learn she can't just pick the first thing she sees.'

Their father pulled his shoes on, whistling. Then he went to his bedroom and fetched his wallet and keys. He piggybacked Samantha all the way to the car, with her singing, 'Giddy-up, Dad!'

Their mother followed sedately, rummaging in her handbag.

They went to the homestead of a Texan, or an ordinary man who might as well have been a Texan, whose advertisement said, 'Horses all types, beg. or exp., 13.1h.h. to 16.3, all purpose, 18mths to 18yrs, suit hacking, western or competition. Also Bedford 3T feed truck, first to see will buy.' Maree took a horse book with all breeds pictured and a series of spot-checks for conformation. But she knew enough, in theory anyway, and staring into a book made her terribly carsick, so she stared out the window instead. For once being carsick did not depress her, and she almost laughed aloud at what she had hitherto occupied herself with on these long drives—imagining a horse of her own running beside the car.

Maree could not help thinking that she would no longer need this wishful dream, therefore she kept her mind off horses.

The car was full of her mother's blown smoke and old lolly wrappers, and the pink driver's side door rattled in a fierce wind. They must have been heard coming for miles.

They pulled up at a pine-lined dusty grove on a narrow bitumen road about two hours from home. Samantha was asleep, and their mother gazed about her in consternation. Among the pine trees, corrals with donkeyish horses sloped outward as though built in a squall.

Pegasus in the Suburbs

Their mother said, 'It looks like, oh, like one of those gypsy camps.' She opened the passenger door but seemed reluctant to climb out. Finally, at a glance from Maree's father, she said, 'Go on, you don't need me to help you choose.'

Maree and her father walked up the driveway. He looked around him as he walked, taking everything in: the truck motors, the pieces of galvanised tin sheeting, the undernourished horses in the corrals. The house was back from the road, surrounded by timber yards and dismantled motor vehicles, and it looked to be made of the sort of material used to make caravans. A half-dozen or so horses dozed placidly behind split logs, and as they got closer the animals' ears twitched.

They reached the corral fences as a man about seven feet tall with a ten-gallon hat was taking a halter off a flea-bitten grey. The horse was thin and rangy and at first glance reminded Maree of a picture she had once seen of a horse's skeleton.

The man said, 'Hey there, g'day.'

Her father greeted him with a pause rather than a specific word, and Maree could tell he was bothered by something to do with either the man or the surroundings.

She piped up, 'Is this the one for sale?' Her father shot her a twitchy look. The horse seemed about to fall over.

The man shrugged. 'Ah,' he said vaguely, 'I got eight, nine, ten for sale, dependin' what y' want. This here's not a bad one, for a start. Over there's her yearlings.' He pointed to a little yard containing two shaggy, stilted beasts with staring ribs. 'But o' course they're not broken in yet. Then there's me cow-roping horses like the two bays in the corner, and a couple of all-purpose ponies y' might like to try out, the chestnut and the taffy. Y' after a Christmas present, eh?'

Maree blushed, and her father said, 'Sort of. Which would you recommend for a girl who hasn't ridden before?'

'Dad, I have ridden before,' Maree reminded him, but he screwed his eyes up irritatedly and waved her away.

The man scratched his head through his hat with a crooked index finger. He looked speculatively at Mr Sterry and said, 'What sort of price range y' talking?'

Maree's father shuffled and his hand in his pocket rattled the car keys back and forth. He said, 'Oh, two, two-fifty if she really finds the right one.'

The man's face registered no impact, though his manner grew slightly breezy. 'Well, at that price, depends on what she wants to do. Like I say, we've still got a few to pick from. See that horse here, that thoroughbred,' (he pointed to a giant stick instect with withers like a dinner plate), 'he's about eighteen years old, y' see. Now, he knows everything there is to know about being ridden, even by a kid who's not much experienced, and apart from that he likes to run, y' won't find a better nag for a girl to start off with.'

Her father said, 'Eighteen, eh.'

Maree whispered, 'Dad, that's too old.' Her forehead was screwed up.

'What about the ponies?' her father said, and Maree frowned harder. A pony was not a horse; it did not convey the same nobility. Though, of course, she would rather have a pony than nothing at all.

'Dad,' she said, 'I'll outgrow it too quickly. I'm fourteen and a half.'

The man fetched the chestnut and the taffy and when

Maree refused a ride, knowing that she was not interested in a pony, he shrugged and put them through some paces. The chestnut skittered and danced. It had wild, frightened eyes and choppy little hooves, and the man's legs hung down so far he looked as though he ought to have worn rollerskates. When he nudged the little creature forward, it fairly bolted and had to be held in check by a perpetual vicelike grip of the reins. After a few minutes, the pseudo-Texan admitted that the chestnut probably needed more work, and swapped to the taffy.

This pony had a shorn mane which stuck up vertically, like a zebra's. Its coat was about an inch long, tufty behind each fetlock, and as it trotted it kept its nose to the air, snuffing the wind. As he rode, the man was saying, 'See, he's a keen little fella, don't do too much wrong, about nine or ten, I guess, done a bit o' campdrafting, so he'll go for just about anything, you name it.' Sliding off over the pony's rump, he said, 'I reckon he's a good sporty horse. You got somewhere to ride?'

Her father said, 'Oh, in the yard, I expect.' He was shifting back and forth from soles to heels, rattling his car keys ominously. Clearly he had not thought much about where Maree would ride the horse, or had assumed the side yard would do.

Maree looked pleadingly from one big man to the other. 'There's a school oval near our place,' she volunteered, 'and a big sort of park place beside the highway. I could take him out there, if he's quiet.'

Her father said, 'Long as you stay off the roads, miss.' He told the salesman where they lived.

Another horse snorted and the taffy pony suddenly put its head down and reared. The man snatched up the reins and flipped them about, still rattling off a list of the animal's traits. 'Runs 'n' jumps, sure, he pig-roots a bit, like any pony, just tryin' to get t' know you.'

Maree said to her father, 'He looks a bit scary.'

Her father grunted in a way that was ambiguous—agreement, or else some combination of distaste and desire to leave.

The man saw their faces. 'Y' want bombproof, like me old brown mare.' He unbuckled the girth and sat the saddle on the fence. The taffy pony galloped away as soon as it was unbridled and settled among the other horses. The man dipped between the rails into the first corral and slapped his hands together, sending horses to either side. The one he ended up with was a big brown animal with a placid expression who allowed herself to be caught and led closer, whereupon Maree and her father saw that her entire face had a jagged vertical scar as though it had once been cracked, and her knees, also, were badly marked.

The man said, 'O'course you'll see she's been in a road smash, probably in a float.' He saddled her and put the bridle on, letting Maree hold the reins. 'Only thing she does wrong is if you get up a canter she'll wheeze a bit like a bad air duct. Not to worry. She's as sound as you or I. Just finds it a bit harder to breathe, 'cause of her accident.'

He gestured invitingly but Maree declined shyly, and with a shrug the cowboy climbed aboard. Gathering up the reins, he booted her hard in the ribs and she gave a small grunt and slowly heaved herself away into the centre of the corral. Every few steps, the man gave her another hefty boot, and just once she broke into a sluggish trot. She had a tendency to wheeze, all right, and every few metres she put her head out and coughed a great, barking cough.

Politely, they watched the man finish his rounds on the coughing mare. After a while she seemed to clear her lungs a little and began to perk up. Then he reined in and offered the horse to Maree. Afraid of injuring the man's feelings by continually rejecting his horses, she gulped and climbed through the rails. She was terrified just approaching the wizened creature. The mare hung her head wheezily, though this was perhaps more in an attempt to snatch at grass below the corral rails than actual distress. The man watched Maree clamber helplessly at the stirrup once or twice, then suddenly he was at her back, cupped hands down at the level of her knee, and face somewhere near her armpit.

The mare sniffed at the attempting rider, and then, playfully almost, she suddenly bared her teeth and nipped the cowboy on the buttock. He jerked back with his elbow right into her muzzle with a pulpy slap and scarcely a glance at her.

Maree felt sorry for the horse but said nothing, and the mare refrained from a second attempt.

'One, two, three!' the man said, and with an upward shove, gripping somewhere on Maree's lower left leg, he had her sky-high and falling into the saddle as though she were trying to vault over instead of settle into it.

The mare grunted and pawed the ground with a fore-hoof.

'Okay,' the man said, slapping her rump, 'off you go. G'wan. Git.' At the same time, Maree gave a tentative nudge in the animal's ribs. The mare's only response was to immediately reef the reins out of Maree's hands.

The man gathered them up and handed them again to Maree. He patiently fed the correct length into her hands and told her to just hang on tight. Then he said, 'Don't be afraid now. Just kick her hard, right behind the girth.'

Obediently she kicked once or twice again, not wishing

to hurt, and the mare did no more than paw the ground. With awesome patience, the man said, 'Try again. This time just give her a real good kick and then keep kicking. Don't let 'er get away with yer.'

Maree kicked the poor stubborn animal as hard as she dared. She was sure she was breaking the mare's rib, at least, or causing some unfathomable interior injury. However, beyond a series of wheezy grunts, the mare refused to budge.

Finally the man had to lead the animal while Maree teetered up high. Even with him jogging beside, giving the mare a sharp slap on the flat of her barrel every few strides, she did no more than lurch into a coughy amble.

Maree said, 'That might be enough now. I don't think she's exactly what I want.'

'Good choice, kiddo,' her father said as she climbed down again.

The man took his hat off his head to wipe his brow. He had lank, sweaty hair in thin, straight locks and a beaky nose. His blue eyes looked blank, like the eyes of a doll in a shop. He said, 'Well, I got one more. It's the grey y' passed when y' came. He's a mite green, though.'

He went in among the horses again and led out a tall, flecked horse. The animal was so bony that his hips appeared abnormally large and his head too big for his neck. Maree blanched. But the horse seemed cooperative enough, occasionally swinging his head underneath to chase a fly from his girth or shoulder while the man applied and adjusted the bridle.

Mr Sterry was eyeing the horse critically as though rehearsing an outright insult. In the world of men, it was up to him to be circumspect. He gave a non-committal 'Ah,' and moved aside to let Maree have a proper look.

Pegasus in the Suburbs

This horse was not at all like those in movies or books. There was no meat on him. The neck was a ewe neck, concave instead of nicely rounded. Maree had looked at so many pictures of champion horses that this looked to be a different kind of animal altogether, like a hyena compared to a lion, rangy and overgrown. Even if he put on some weight, he would always look nondescript.

Her throat prickled. She had desperately wanted a horse from this visit. Because she wanted a horse so badly, any horse, she said, 'He's not so bad. He just needs feeding.' And having said this, she convinced herself it was true.

Her father shrugged a little and said, 'Your choice, kiddo, I said that already.' They were talking side-of-the-mouth, as though in conspiracy.

The horse stood quietly while the man lifted his hooves, slapping each heavily with a giant palm, and all the time rattling off a series of incomprehensible points about his wind and strength. Clinging to optimism, Maree saw that the gelding had mild, dark eyes that looked everywhere with quiet interest. When the man reefed his muzzle apart they could see small, flat, even teeth and no bridle tooth behind his incisors. The man said, 'See here, he's a three-year-old. Y' get 'em older and they get this big tusky fang about here.' He pointed to the blank space on the gum where eventually a pointed tooth should emerge. Maree nodded, watching him, feeling suddenly the depth of her lack of knowledge.

As they listened, Maree found it easier to focus on the horse's good points, such as the hint of Arabian in his face's faint curve. She remembered reading that if you make a horse arch his neck to feed, he always gets a more pleasing topline.

She looked to her father for some suggestion of his mood, but he looked worried, displeased. His hand moved in his pocket, jingle-jangling keys and coins the way he always did when he was fed up with a situation. She had the sudden mortifying notion that she would come away from today without a horse at all.

She said, 'Um, he's lovely,' trying to will herself to think so.

The man was already talking again. 'He's a quiet one for a green horse, but he's also got fire. He can run all day, he can pull up on a twenty-cent piece, he can neck-rein, he lunges, you'll win everything you go in—campdrafting, cross-country, calf-roping, you name it.' He threw a towel over the horse's back, forgetting to raise the fold a little so that saddling would not tighten the fabric unbearably over the horse's spine. The horse's pale slender mouth fretted over the bit, which was, Maree knew from books, a Spanish snaffle. The bridle had no noseband and the cheekstrap was a piece of hay-string tied too loosely and slipped casually over the animal's head. The saddle was a high-pommel stock saddle with semicircular knee pads.

Maree had drawn horses with saddles, horses without saddles, and every type of bit and bridle combination possible. She had drawn horses being ridden over jumps and horses being ridden through water, under rain, or thundering along with foals at foot and sunlight beaming down. She had drawn the Man from Snowy River plunging his mount down a landslide and Obsidian the famous racehorse, standing in a show ring about to be awarded his champion ribbon.

Nothing had prepared her for this angular beast.

In order to wish for him, she had to imagine him in a kind of future, a horse-in-becoming. However, even as she decided to like the grey, her father began to seem less indifferent and more outrightly annoyed. Every few minutes he cleared his throat and emitted a gravelly 'Hrrrr.' For him, perhaps, it was status; an ugly horse would suggest to the neighbours a poor outlay. He might not have wanted to spend much, but he certainly wanted the appearance of value.

The lean, grey ghost-horse was intermittently swallowed in dust, and at other times, as he passed, he brushed the fence where her father stood. The cowboy turned him at a twitch of the reins, which were so loose that they made giant swinging arcs down to his chest. He pressed the horse on and on in its bony, jolting paces.

Maree crossed her legs and bit one salty thumb. She said to her father, eagerly, 'He seems to go well,' thinking about the horse she'd ridden with Danielle at the riding farm, which had not particularly wanted to deviate in the rider's chosen direction at all.

The man drew up in front of them and drawled, 'He'll spin, he'll side-pass, he's not afraid o' cows, he'll tie up 'n float, he's no problem with other horses, you can leave 'im all day in the sun and he won't drink, hooves no problem, he don't eat much, just a biscuit o' lucerne once a day in winter, he's just one of those horses that don't need much feed. If you want to show 'im, well, just give 'im time to come off stockwork and you can retrain easy, better to get a horse that's done the hard work early so he knows who's boss.' And more in similar vein.

Maree's father said to her, 'I don't know, pet. I can't imagine him fitting in that side yard. I don't want you riding a horse that size in traffic: you might get hit by a car, who knows what.'

Maree gushed, 'But he looks quiet, and I'll ride him at a walk, it's safer than leading.'

Her father gave her an obscure look. He said to the cowboy, 'How quiet is he in traffic?'

The man paused, scratching his head under the browband of his hat. 'Quiet, like she said. If you let a bomb go off underneath 'im, well, he's like anybody, but my daughter's been riding him on the road and he's pretty road-smart. But the main thing is he won't bolt or chuck you off, he's the sort of horse'll take a little jump and then just stand there, look around to see what the noise was, and half a second later he's back in stride. He won't care about trucks or buses or whatnot. Like I said, he's a tame one, just a bit green. He's got a good heart, just not much experience.'

Maree's father made a small sound, neither agreement nor disagreement.

The man slid off the horse's back like a length of steel siding off a delivery truck. He ducked under the animal's belly from both sides to show them how sedate he was. He pulled the tail to either side, and through all of this the horse neither kicked nor moved away, but yawned massively.

Maree said, 'I think I'd like to have a ride.' The man beamed, so string-beany that even a smile caused his face to widen, and he passed her the reins.

Again she clambered through the corral rails. In the vicinity of the horse she almost changed her mind, since he was so much taller than the mare. Eventually the man stooped to once more boost her into the saddle, and she knew she could not back out.

It took three attempts because she had trouble getting her centre of gravity high enough to reach the top. When she did sit down, everything felt so wobbly she was sure she was going to fall off, especially since the horse had already made a few shuffling steps forward. Then, before she could gather the reins, the horse was trotting toward the corral centre at some subtle signal her shifting body had imparted, and she felt her untrained body slacking back and forth until some of her remembered book lessons about posture asserted themselves over her unaccustomed muscles and she gathered some slack out of the rein loops. At least she knew not to stick her elbows out. The man wove himself into the corral rails and stood in the background, some seller's instinct telling him to shut up.

The ride was exhilarating, fierce and terrifying. She thought at each jerky step that she would lose balance, but with the assistance of the kneepads, she stayed in the saddle. From up high the ewe neck seemed impossibly slender, the mane shorn right back to the roots so that bald black skin showed through. The neckline looked to be all sinew, as though the animal were just skin stretched over bone. Behind the saddle, the loins were a raised streak curving into bony hips, which finished in an undernourished rump. But through the saddle's stiff, thick leather and all around her she felt the warm, toned health of a creature that loved to move, all his muscles and ribcage ready for directional alteration or sudden flight. The mouth was surprisingly pliant: tightening a rein produced so sharp a turn that she realised she would be safer to neck-rein. He halted fidgetingly the moment she sat deep into the saddle, and moved forward almost at a leap when she clicked her tongue. Any expression at all from her seemed to produce an instant response.

Maree rode for perhaps five minutes, ever conscious of the possibility of falling. But immediately after she had dismounted, what had been fear was replaced by a surge of hope that eclipsed everything and made her believe she had thoroughly enjoyed the ride. This must be what it would feel like to have climbed a really tall mountain or fought some long and terrible battle.

'Dad,' she pleaded, trying to sound calm, 'he's really good to ride, he's got a soft mouth. I like him.'

Maree's father was still unimpressed. 'He's got a soft mouth, has he?' He turned to the lanky cowboy, who was picking his teeth, and said, 'She thinks she knows every-thing from one lesson at some riding ranch.'

Maree blushed. She looped the reins onto the fence. The horse snuffed at her palm and his lips were as soft as velvet. He seemed taller and more angular than a crane.

Her father was shifting from foot to foot. He said finally, 'Well, it's up to you.' She had never realised before how definitely this indicated his displeasure with some-thing. His displeasure was like an undertow in a brook. To risk crossing was usually to drown.

Gulping, she plunged in. 'Dad, can we buy him?'

Her father reflected.

The cowboy broke in helpfully, 'What tack have you got?'

Maree's father's lower lip began to quiver, a sure sign that he was meditating negatively on a situation. It was the pose he adopted in front of the television when his team had bungled a goal or hit a ball into the hands of a wicket-keeper. Finally he said, 'Not much, to tell the truth.'

The man scratched his head through his hat. Sweat trickled to either side of his brow, and his jaw was clenched. He did a quick mental calculation and then said, 'Well, I guess I could throw in a couple of other things as well.'

Maree touched her father's arm. He was listening, head slightly to one side. He said, 'What have you got?'

'I'll chuck in the bridle he's got on. It's not anything fancy, but it works.'

'Dad?' Maree started, and he glanced at her and away. He said to the cowboy, 'What's it likely to cost us to buy a saddle?'

There was an angular shrug and the man gave a laconic exhalation while he thought. 'Tell you what,' he said at last, 'I ain't got too many spare saddles, but up the back there's a basic unit I don't use all that often. I could let you have that for, oh, sixty, seventy, and two for the horse and bridle and whatnot.'

Mr Sterry said, 'So we'd be looking at, what, two hundred and sixty, say?'

'Yeah, I guess.'

Maree held her breath. A horse, bought for her, would be hers more than anything else she had ever had. Living outside the house, it would automatically be in a different jurisdiction. It would be responsive to her. Deftly now, she imagined the horse filling out, growing solid, the muscles forming rounded hillocks underneath his flecked hide, his proud neck arched as they galloped along, mane and tail trailing.

The cowboy, with a salesman's sixth sense for timing, began needlessly counting bonuses on his fingers. 'You'll never need to shoe him unless you're going to pony club. These horses came off desert country and their feet have never needed shoes, you just trim 'em once a month or two and paint a bit of linseed on 'em. Listen, I'll throw in a free bag of oat hulls, they just came in yesterday and I've got plenty. Take 'em. What do you want, Sunday delivery? Saturday? I'll be up over your way gearing up for an

115

auction. I'll float him across. That way you get him before Christmas.'

Maree looked at her father and swallowed anything in her that might hold out for something better. Noting her expression he suddenly grinned. 'I did say it was your choice,' he said.

Maree said, 'I'll be happy!' and her father relented. He ruffled her hair and said by way of explanation or apology, 'She's a strong-headed kid, this one. I guess this is the horse for her, then.' Somewhat reluctantly, he reached for his wallet.

The man started unsaddling, tossing the reins over the fence rail with the casualness of a clinched sale. The horse mouthed the bit non-stop until the man undid the throat-latch and pulled the bridle off. Then the horse walked stiffly away, all hips and sinew and saddle-sweat.

Two hundred and sixty dollars moved into the seller's dusty hands and seemed to disappear. He went off to get a receipt.

Maree said in the new nervous silence, 'He'll come good. I'll look after him, Dad. I'll do extra work around the house to make up for his feed.'

Maree's father laughed and clutched her to his side in a clumsy attempt at a hug. He said, 'What do you mean, extra? I'd buy you a herd of horses, pet. Remember, no more skipping meals, and you keep your mother happy.'

Maree bowed her head in mute acquiescence. No promise seemed too great to make in return for this horse. In the corral, horses that weren't hers whickered and whinnied. She fought the desire to scan them once again, to see if they were better than the one her father had finally purchased, while the tall grey horse nosed his way around the corral and then let himself down on his knees and began to roll. Dust flew and entered their mouths, their hair and sinuses, caking father and daughter. Mr Sterry cleared his throat and glanced at his watch.

Just then Maree's mother came up the driveway holding Samantha's hand. She was yawning and blinking, looking around vaguely. Samantha said, 'Daddy, look what I stepped in.' Her left sandal was edged with green.

Maree's mother said, 'Sshh,' and twitched Sam's arm. Then she looked at Maree curiously, without rancour. She said, 'Well?' and let Sam go to pick at some weed flowers beside the driveway.

The horse arched his rump as though to demonstrate what he thought of Maree's ability to choose, or her mother's question, or both, then tucked himself under and let down a giant penisworth of piss, groaning and farting into the horsey air.

Maree's mother waved a hand distastefully in front of her nose. She appeared genuinely shocked. Perhaps she sensed some pact: the horse, her husband and Maree.

Mr Sterry stared into the middle distance until the man came back with a sparkle and a witty side-step. He handed over a bit of paper and tipped his hat to Maree's mother, who put her hand to her upper chest in surprise.

'Done,' the men said, and shook hands.

All eyes were on Maree. 'What's his name?' she said, not that she cared, as she would call him what she chose.

'Tell the truth,' the man said, 'he just gets called the grey. Got too many horses, as you can see. Damn things are worse than chickens.'

High neighs filled the dustbowls beyond the house. Mrs Sterry seemed to come to herself briefly enough to exclaim, 'Oh, you have chickens!' Nobody could have imagined that she would exclaim over chickens. Aware of having surprised herself as well as her family, she looked about on the ground as though hunting for eggs. Then Samantha got bitten by an ant and arrested the situation with a childish squall.

Maree felt the mortification only a teenage girl in the clasp of her family can feel.

The cowboy waved them all on their way with promises to deliver on Saturday. His belt buckle was a steer's head with horns, and as he watched them walk back down the driveway he hooked it with both thumbs.

All the way home Maree was trying to think of a name. Spitfire. Wildfire. Gelignite. Geronimo. Jupiter. Firefly. Bonjour. Freckles.

Her father had his lips pursed, visible in the corner of the rear-view mirror. Her mother was awake now, tense with motion and traffic lights, dinner to be got ready, cleaning and preparations to be done. The end of possibilities, homecoming.

Quite suddenly, and with a pent-up force, Maree's mother said, 'And now, I don't even need to say this, it's not even an issue, you're going to have a spotless bedroom every time either myself or your father happen to come past. Not just today, not just for Christmas, but forever.' Having said that, she sat back in her seat, triumphant, and something like a better mood evolved in the air around her. By the time they turned into their street, only her father was taciturn, and he was probably merely concerned about the cost.

Maree thought, Diamond. Barb. Sting. Aquarius. Sandman. Flipper. Ben. Salty. Lassie. Rin Tin Tin.

Maree was a girl who owned a horse.

ELEVEN

Danielle knew everything, it seemed, about horses. Yet even she did not yet have one of her own. When Maree told her, she was full of prim dignity and asked questions like 'So does he have a pedigree? Any papers at all? What do you think he is, Anglo-Arab?'

Maree agreed nervously. 'Yeah, he looks Anglo.'

Her friend had a bossy nature that found good outlet here, and generously gave Maree important instructions relating to feeding and shoeing. Danielle told her that the riding ranch also sold hay and other horse feed, and if Maree wanted she would come with her to buy tack. 'Of course you know you can't ride him on the road until you get some shoes on him, or else he'll get splints,' she warned. 'And of course you have to pick his feet out every morning, without fail, or he might get a fungus and have to be put down.'

Maree promised to do everything she was told. From that conversation alone, she took a page of notes. Although many of the books she had read were about the care of horses, she'd skimmed these daily elements for the more fanciful information, such as the history of the Arab, the flight of Lippizaners. Daily care was usually mentioned in terms of mucking out a stable and plaiting mane and tail. Maree's family certainly had no stable, and she had not thought to purchase a comb or brush. Having no money of her own, that manner of thinking was slow to occur.

She squirrelled away an old plastic brush, one of Lissa's many defunct hairbrushes, and a number of old towels she thought she could use as saddle-blankets.

On Saturday morning, Maree's father collared her at eight o'clock and said, 'So what are we going to do about that side yard, eh?' He was standing with his head inside the bedroom and body out in the hall, tucked around the wall. It was as though his daughters' bedroom made him insecure.

Maree had been in bed, not sleeping but thinking about her horse. Having been woken, Lissa was groaning at them and turning her face to the wall. As Maree climbed out of bed, Lissa pulled her pillow over her head.

Maree dressed in cut-off jeans and emerged in the kitchen. Her father's face wore a kind of mute fury, the pall of domesticity and its labours heavy on him. Mowing or the odd washing-up chore had this effect on him, as though, out in his weekday labours, only tasks of honour or dignity were assigned him. Yet he had been a labourer, bowser mechanic, salesman. He had dug into bare earth with blistered hands.

At the sink, her mother was watering some sunflower seeds she had poked into wads of cotton wool. She said, not looking at them, 'What are you pair up to?'

Maree said, joking darkly, since she was getting her horse today and nothing else mattered, 'A wigwam for a goose's bridal.'

Her mother looked at her blankly for a moment as her father, stepping outside, said irritably over his shoulder, 'We're cleaning up the paddock!' Shrugging, Maree's mother went back to her sunflowers.

When Maree went outside, her father was already in the side yard, where the grass was a knee-high tangle. Among it, boots met near-invisible obstacles of steel piping and sheets of galvanised iron. Old plant pots, their plastic decayed in the sun, cracked underfoot. Maree spent half an hour picking pieces out of the grass and putting them in a garbage bag while her father paced the yard, as he had done when considering an extension to the house. A washing-machine bowl, rusted to the earth, resounded at his hefty kick.

Maree said helpfully, 'That could be a feeding bin. We could stand it upright in a corner.'

He grunted. Samantha, playing with a scooter along the length of the backyard, tried to bring it through the fence. The handlebars stuck. Maree could hear her mother in the house yelling at Samantha to come inside, but the little girl was determined to join the grown-ups.

Mr Sterry said to Maree, 'Stack these bricks.' He began to sweat and swear at bits of wood. Maree timidly began picking up old housebricks so embedded in earth they had to be wrenched free of thickened grass that grew up through the holes and down into the soil in fat white roots. Shiny black creatures scurried or slimed on her fingertips. By some miracle she was not bitten by a funnelweb spider, for there were a great many suspicious-looking webby holes.

Jennifer Kremmer

Her father dragged long sheets of metal into a pile and tied them together with clothesline. Tin made thundery sounds. Samantha came back out to help or get in the way, outfitted by her mother in a tied-up apron and a straw sunbonnet. She marched toward Maree like a soldier, chiming, 'Daddy, Maree, look at me!' The scooter lay forgotten, half in and half out of the paling gate.

Touched by her sister's wish to help, Maree set Samantha to piling up pieces of plastic, but the little girl soon forgot what she had come out there for, and began digging holes in the earth.

Mr Sterry moved the car to just out front of the side yard. When he had first bought this lot , he had made some show of fencing the front with the same plumber's piping as now graced their front yard; due to a shortage of materials he had ended with star-posts. As a final indignity, this fence had been given a bed frame, steel-meshed, as its gate. The grass around this makeshift gate had grown so long that, try as he might, he could not get the thing open.

Swearing and rubbing his forehead, he kicked at the long grass. 'Where's your mother?' he asked Maree.

'Inside.'

'Go ask her if she knows where the hedge clippers are.'

Maree did. Her mother came out onto the back steps wiping her hands on a tea-towel. Her face registered a sort of uninterested anxiety. She muttered, 'What am I, his toolkit?' Together they found the hedge clippers at the back of the laundry cupboard, brown blades fused with rust. It was hard to imagine them performing any serious clipping.

Maree's mother found a rusty can of rust-loosener and they spent five minutes going over the blades with a steel-wool pad and the oily spray. Her mother straightened up and said, 'They still won't open, but here you go.' She

122

gave a tiny glance of near-conspiracy, which Maree hugged to herself, then the girl hurried off with the clippers.

Her father never mowed lawn unless it became such an eyesore that it overcame his domestic unwillingness. At the same time, the sensation of grass against his ankles or trousers irritated him beyond measure, and Maree had seen him fume his way into the home of an evening with his eyebrows drawn in a furrow because of the grass. Their front yard, of all the houses in the street, suffered most from a sense of overgrowth; always there was this green, spongy mass inching its way up the bricks and over the paths. As he bent over at the side fence and pulled and kicked at the voluminous mess he looked like madman who could find nothing better to do than wrestle with nature, to his own cost. When Maree got closer, he held his hands out for the shears, without taking his eyes off the offending patch.

He tried to open them once, then looked at her so piercingly she cringed.

'Bloody morons!' he groaned, out of all reasonableness. This was her father on his worst of days. His face was dripping from effort. He wiped his forearm across his forehead and appealed to the sky. 'When I asked for the grass clippers, did I have to specify a pair that worked?'

Maree said nervously, 'I didn't know we had any others.'

He ignored her and set to with bare hands once more, pulling masses of grass and earth up in great clutches and swinging them backward, where they piled up near the car. In this manner he was eventually able to budge the gate and, though it cost the lower wire hinge, force it wide open.

Samantha had given up all pretence of helping. She

crouched near the car's rear tyre, piling small street pebbles in mounds.

Her father hauled tin sheets toward the car. Eventually it was loaded with green plastic garbage bags full of old pots, twisted wire, paper rubbish, cans, and rotting wood with nails. The roof racks were stacked with tin. They had not cleaned the yard completely, but what remained was innocuous enough, and at least, unlike the galvanised tin, not likely to injure an animal.

Samantha had gone to stand on the verandah, idly following one way or another. She said loudly, 'I wanna go too.'

Her father ignored her. Climbing into the driver's seat, he seemed to be calmer now. Finally he said, 'All right, then,' and gestured toward Maree's knee, where she was to sit.

The pink driver's side door rattled all the way to the tip. At the entrance, a man in a singlet waved them along a rutted clay road past a vast desolate scrape of dirt, the whole lot overseen by seagulls. A salty, fetid wind reached the car and Samantha kept flapping her hand at her face and saying, 'Phew, it stinks!' until her father said, 'Give it a rest!'

Maree and her father climbed out and together swung bags over the drop with a stiff camaraderie; she was constantly afraid she would do something to offend him and this made her clumsy, dropping garbage bags so that they split, and losing her half of the load too quickly so that it landed at their feet instead of over the edge.

Mr Sterry hauled out pieces of steel and the galvanised sheeting by himself, saying, 'I'll do it, I'll do it,' when she tried to help and got her hand pinched. There was nothing else to do.

Samantha kicked around in the dirt looking for anything interesting. She already had a doll's head and a pretty, blue-flowered tin teapot, only mildly rusty. Her fingernails were orange with clay.

Maree leaned against the car with her arms crossed. A man driving a yellow ute with a black dog chained to the back said, 'Hoi there,' and winked. His face was crinkled with good humour and his biceps were brown and knotty.

Startled, she looked away, but sneaked a final look as the ute reversed.

He winked again as he drove off.

Her father came back, wiping his forehead against the back of his gloves. Rust had stained his forearms in dull russet tiger-stripes. Maree suspected he'd seen the man winking at her and she began talking nervously 'Oh, Dad, you should see what Samantha's found, it's a teapot.' But the look of curious annoyance on his face told her to stop. He took the pot out of Samantha's hands, slapped some of the dirt from her and said, 'In the car, kids.'

Samantha knew not to cry, though her face was pinched.

Now that the labour was done, their father grew almost festive. He pointed out peculiar shapes in trees and clouds as he drove, and even pulled up at a service station and bought Maree and Samantha lime ice-blocks with creamy insides. They ate in a new and well-earned peace.

Maree's mother was watering lilacs when they pulled into the drive; Lissa was standing on the front verandah smiling into the sun with cucumber pieces taped over her eyes. Her father said, 'What are you doing, idiot girl?' as he passed, but he was jovial and did not wait for a reply. In a few minutes, he had settled into his recliner with a newspaper and was deeply engrossed.

Each time Samantha walked by, he patted her head. These were the unpredictabilities of their father.

Lissa did not remove her cucumbers, she just said in Maree's direction, 'Has he been on the warpath again?'

Maree shrugged and went into the bedroom. After her exertion she was too excited to sit down, or even begin another picture, and so she stood at the window for the next hour or so listening for the truck.

Samantha came into the bedroom wearing a Catwoman cape made of black shiny plastic. 'Ta-da,' she announced, 'look what Mum got me.'

But the sound Maree had been waiting for arrived; the street rumbled with a truck. Maree brushed Samantha out of the way with a murmured, 'Oh, wow, that's great, Sam,' and was already on the verandah when the horse truck came into view.

The cowboy, minus his hat, was harried, laconic, businesslike and abrupt in illogical turns. He unloaded the bridle, feed bag, saddle, and the giant grey horse that looked even skinnier than before, all with bustling efficiency. The saddle was ancient. It was dingy grey and the stirrup irons were flecked with rust, but none of that mattered in the moment; she took it from him with a smile. He'd also swapped the bridle he had intended to give them for an ancient mould-peppered contraption with an eroded bit. Maree didn't care; she just hoped her father would not notice anything wrong, for she was afraid he would tell the man to take the purchases back and return their cash.

'Put 'im in 'ere?' the cowboy said doubtfully of the front yard, which was just big enough for the horse to move about six paces each way, and Maree's father, standing on the verandah with his arms crossed, said, 'The side yard, mate. There's a gate out front.'

Pegasus in the Suburbs

Maree stopped patting the horse's neck to say, 'I'll get it.' Curious thrills turned her legs to a runner's legs; she could have won any race at school, had she been able to recall this heady spurt. Racing on behalf of her horse, she flew.

A little way behind Maree, the cowboy said, 'Whoa!' as the horse baulked at his new home. Maree lifted the bed frame heavily over the bared earth. The big grey pranced at the end of the reins, uncertain about whether to enter the yard at all. It took a hard slap in the flank before he moved forward with such a lurch that the cowboy said, 'Oi, smart-arse!' When he had the gate secured and the bridle off the horse's head he said, 'He's a mild one, that, just got a bit of wind up.'

The horse nosed around the paddock. There were great patches of yellow-rooted soil where tin and other junk had been removed; it looked as though Maree's family had started to build something and stopped at the foundations. Her father came up behind them and scratched his head.

The cowboy handed Maree the bridle, waved nonchalantly and hopped back in his truck. The windowpanes shook as he drove away.

After a moment, Maree's father said, 'I'll say this for you, daughter, you can pick an ugly one.' He stood with his arms crossed, watching the horse snatch at kikuyu and occasionally tear away whole earthy clumps. Mr Sterry's expression was pained, as though the horse somehow added to the unsightliness of the place, in a way that the overgrown scattered tin and the old bed-frame gate did not. Not speaking, he went back to the house.

Maree gazed at her horse with a strange mixture of headiness and horror. The animal was spectacularly unkempt. His withers stuck out along the top of his back

127

like a butte on a plain. Each sprung rib caged a taut musculature so lean it was like fabric, like a vast sheet stretched over a ribbed panel. When his hind legs moved in their lanky toe-drag, the sinews in his hips formed lines and arcs and the hollow at his flank enlarged. He was a creature of lines and pocks.

She hurried off to fetch him some feed. The bag of oat hulls that the cowboy had promised was leaning against the verandah. Maree found a bucket in the laundry and took a pair of scissors out the front, but when she opened the hessian sack she saw that the hulls were flat and greenish and stinking of mildew. Clumps of them were webbed together by weevils.

It was nearly five, too late in the day to buy hay anywhere, and Danielle had told her that the riding ranch, which also acted as a fodder supplier, only delivered on Thursdays. Maree leaned on the gate watching her horse sample the rough grass. The more he ate, the rounder and more pleasing he would grow. Every mouthful made her hopeful he would fill out. But the kikuyu carried strips of earth and the horse was impatient and prone to spitting it out.

The front yard of the house gave Maree an idea. Rarely mowed, it had endured her mother's overwatering with a lush sort of contempt. The grass had never been subjected to the rusting hulks of old washing tubs or galvanised tin sheets, and was thick and green, like grass was supposed to be. Maree snatched up great lush handfuls of it, depositing them over the palings, and the horse eventually ambled over to eat. She went on until her arms ached and her hands were lime-green.

Maree's mother came to stand on the verandah, her face

all concern. She'd done her hair in rollers and was stuffing the evidence under a pale scarf.

'He's big for a small yard,' she said, not unkindly.

Maree shrugged. She was still thinking of names. Bell. Trance. Hemingway. Diamante. Callistemon. Samantha kept coming out onto the verandah to point and shout while her mother fixed a piece of the Catwoman cape that had torn. While Maree picked grass, Samantha called out, 'Is he fierce?'

Grunting with effort, Maree said, 'Not really fierce, but you better not come too close because I don't know if he bites or kicks, and sometimes little kids get in the way and you wouldn't want a hoofprint in your forehead.'

'A what? A what?'

'You wouldn't want a kick in the head.'

Maree's mother led the girl inside.

Then Mr Sterry came to see how she was progressing. He was halfway through a leg-ham sandwich, now in his weekend singlet and shorts. Maree could hear his jaw clicking even from across the yard. He said, loud through his mouthful, 'Wouldn't feed a dog off that carcass, eh Maree.'

Angrily, she flushed, even though she knew he was trying to be placatory. Sometimes she truly hated her father. Sometimes she wished him dead, trampled by a giant horse into the dirt. She turned and ignore him.

He watched her for a while, then went back to the cricket, jaws clicking with each judgemental, thoughtless chomp.

When he had gone, Maree leaned as far as possible over the palings and watched her horse eat. He seemed contented, although her face above the fence seemed to cause him some concern, for every now and then he snorted and turned as though to walk away, watching Maree intently. Each time, the grass pile drew him back to nibble more. Although she had picked masses of grass, in five minutes he had eaten it all and wandered away to other parts of the yard. She began to worry that he would not find enough to eat among the wiry stuff of the paddock.

It occurred to her that she could leave him in the house yard for a couple of hours. Certainly, hand-picking was laborious and inefficient, for the horse ate far more quickly than she was able to provide. In the front yard the piping fence was high enough to keep him in, and although the yard was small, the grass was plentiful and not too stringy or tough. Humming softly, Maree examined the bridle. It was tangled from being looped over a fence, but finally, sorting pieces of leather, she worked out which end was which.

She climbed the bed-frame gate, and the horse swivelled his ears. Sleepy eyes stared past her, looking for sources of threat or escape. He stopped chewing to reflect on her presence. Then, lurching slightly, he turned shoulder on and walked away.

This surprised her, as the horse seller had had no such trouble. Maree said, 'Hey there, lovely,' overly conscious of her words, so that her voice sounded hollow yet full of guile. Every now and then he would put his head down and snatch at more grass, but as soon as she got close he would spring into a high-minded walk in the opposite direction.

Maree was flummoxed. Finally she had the brainwave of picking a great fistful of good grass from the front yard and approaching the horse with it. She stopped about three metres away, waving her offering, with the bridle behind her back.

Pegasus in the Suburbs

The horse snuffed, nostrils flared. His head came forward to the limit of his neck, then he took a hesitant step in her direction. When his soft lips began to muzzle the grass, she took the opportunity to sling the reins up over his neck, and in this manner she held him.

Once the reins were around his throat, he gave her a surly glance but made no attempt to escape. Maree stood there with the bridle in her hands, trying to work out how to put it on him.

She raised the bit to his teeth and scrabbled it lightly past the lips, but each time he clamped his teeth and shook his head from side to side. She could not think what she was doing wrong. In books, the horses always put their heads forward to take the bit. In the cowboy's corral, the bridle had been mysteriously whipped in place so quickly that she had simply accepted its placement as fact, as had the horse.

'Come on,' she kept saying, wobbling the metal. He simply refused, and in the end jerked his head high each time she made the attempt.

Maree was standing there with the horse in reins and no way of working out how to complete bridling him. At least when she tried to lead him forward by the reins he obliged at the pressure on his neck. It was only when she clacked the bit against his teeth that, clenched, he shook her off.

Just then Lissa stuck her head over the palings, sucking on a raspberry frozen tube. She was on a pre-adult cusp in which raspberry tubes had as much place as the tongue-kisses at the back of the school weathershed that she often told Maree about. Maree, three years younger, had never voluntarily put her face within two feet of a boy, and she never knew what to say when Lissa recounted her amorous

131

escapades, beyond a painfully reticent 'Wow. Did you really?'

The horse baulked slightly, then recovered. In his belly, grass chewings made a gaseous murmur.

Lissa said, keeping well covered and with a pained expression, 'He's pretty skinny, isn't he Ree? Aren't they meant to look sort of round?'

Incensed, Maree snapped, 'How would you know?'

Her older sister's face grew reserved. 'How are we going to feed him, hey?' It was the sort of question that sounded as though there had been discussion behind doors. It was exactly her mother's voice.

With disquiet, Maree scowled back. 'I'll take him out every day to let him graze. And I'll get a job if I have to, and leave school. There's nothing to learn there anyway, except how to kiss boys.'

Lissa sucked the raspberry, mouth as red as the ice. 'Don't be a moron all your life,' she said in perfect Father-tone. 'You can't leave school, you've got to get your HSC first. Or do you think you can just sail through the world on your pony?'

'Suppose I've got to learn how to suck a boy's dick, too,' Maree said under her breath.

They stared at each other. Raspberry ice slid into syrup at the bottom of the plastic tube. It was an odd moment because they rarely fought, and Lissa by nature was, as Maree knew, kind. But because this was their first fight in a while, there were no proper rules.

Lissa said, 'At least I'll never be sucking a horse's dick,' and disappeared.

Fuming, Maree kicked at a clump of roots, and the sudden motion spooked the horse. He settled again and snuffed warily at her fingers with his great soft nose.

Whiskers and warm breath tickled her palm. Heartened, she used the reins over his neck to lead him to the front fence; he came more or less willingly, occasionally ducking his head against the leather restraint to shoo a fly from his chest.

Maree undid the gate and carefully, holding the reins very tightly, moved the horse backward at the same time as she dragged the gate open into the paddock. He was wary, but placid. Then she started to lead him out to take him into the front yard.

But just then something plasticky came rustling along the footpath. It was Samantha, shrieking, 'Hey, Maree, look at me now! I'm a Catwoman again!' She leaped, a sudden apparition enveloped in black, through the ratty grass toward the horse.

The horse's spine buckled and he lurched forward with such force that Maree was carried along for several feet, her own feet dragging on the ground. She hung on, shouting at Samantha to stay away, desperately trying to keep the animal from kicking or trampling her. Then all at once, with a sickening and mould-weakened *thuck*, the reins snapped about six inches from her hand, and she slipped backward and landed hard on her coccyx.

The bridle with its snapped reins landed at her feet, completely free of the horse.

Snorting in terror, the grey swung his gangly bulk into the centre of the bitumen road. Farting horsily, unshod hooves skittering, he began his nimble, athletic gallop into disappearance. Maree, in tears of anguish and indignity, snatched up the bridle and, followed by the cries and insults and pleas of her kin, began her impossible pursuit.

TWELVE

Her father was shouting at her to come back. Samantha had set up one of her high, shrill wails. Maree didn't care. She was terrified a car would turn up at any moment and hit the horse, or the horse hit it—any number of catastrophes could befall a horse and a car. The bridle her only link to the animal careering ahead, dangled uselessly from her hand.

Her dash in his wake made the horse even more spooked. He kept to the centre of the road, stick-legs flailing out behind him. From the rear an escaping nag is a foolish sight, a gigantic bottom with a minuscule sideward-peering head. Maree hated her new horse just then, seeing him from that angle, in the way that primitive people might have hated the outline of the escaping deer on which they had wasted their last arrowhead. Every now and then he would slow, spin and then sprint off again in an awkward, spindly canter that soon reverted to a jaunty and alert quickstep. He crossed the road, turned, baulked, and continually drew further ahead. Finally he crossed a main thoroughfare and, galloping along a nature strip on the other side, disappeared from view between some trees.

With a pain in her coccyx, Maree felt her features dissolving into unheroic sobs. Hatred toward Samantha rose in her gut, and in order not to collapse with it, she fragmented the hate and applied it to everybody and everything. She hated the suburb and its horse-stealing streets and front yards. She hated her father for deriding her choice of horse and for having a jaw that clicked when he ate. She hated Lissa for reminding her that at the back of every gift was a little sea of expectation and potential for punishment.

It was her mother, of all surprises, who caught up with her first. Maree was gasping too hard to continue running and had slowed to a disconsolate walk. She was so upset she barely heard the stumble of feet in her wake. Her mother was wearing a hastily thrown-on pink overshirt and sneakers. She clutched at her chest in distress. Maree despised her for the pink overshirt and for being the breeder of Samantha. Ignorant of this, her mother rambled breathlessly, 'What will he do, where will he go, oh, where is he, did you see where he went?' in a series of pointless exasperations.

Maree said, 'How the hell should I know?'

Maree's mother flapped and almost tripped over. In her hands was a blue-and-white checkered tea-towel. 'Oh, Maree,' she cried, 'get in the car when your father comes along and go straight to the police station and report it. Your father will know what to do. Where can a horse run to, how far can he go?'

Maree became accusing. 'Why was I born? Why didn't you just kill me?'

Her words hung in the air and her mother stopped in shock, all the worry leaving her face for a numb instant. She waved the tea-towel emptily by her side in a flap.

'You—you ungrateful girl!' she gasped. All her air left her and she appeared to collapse inward like an empty bag. The vast accumulation of her daily sorrow seemed to leak out. Then, white in the face and trembling, she turned back the way she'd come, shaking her head.

Maree kept walking. She was thinking of all the times she had packed her school bag with clothes and fallen asleep, only to wake in the morning forgetful of the intention behind her act. Why could she never remember to run away? Why this daily torture and night-time fantasy?

She was imagining that she could leave the suburb, work as a stable-sweeper, ride racehorses, win races, be given one of the failed champions as a parting gift from a generous owner.

While she was in this mixed muse, Samantha's face, fatuously cherubic, rose gleefully in front of Maree, so that at times she raged and at others merely marched along with her eyes blurred with tears. At the bottom of the street, large women with aprons and slippers stood on the footpath staring along the roadway, mouths open. Their eyes glanced over her, connected A to B and pointed her in the right direction. Maree said nothing, but marched off in her own fog of dismay. The women muttered after her.

She would never go back home. She would sleep out under the stars on a rugged mountaintop with a harmonica and a white dog, occasionally begging for sustenance from valley farms. Every few steps she made a new, violent departure plan and quickly despised herself for not taking it up.

The blue Ford station wagon with one pink panel drove up behind her, its horn beeping shrilly. Maree's father leaned over and wound the passenger side window down.

She moved toward the door, but made no attempt to get in. Her father was refusing to look directly at her, and Maree had the sudden intuition that her father considered her entirely at fault. She knew this as soon as she looked at his face. He blamed her for losing the horse because he blamed her for getting that particular horse in the first place.

All this knowledge was revealed in his upright, affectedly nonchalant posture.

Maree said, 'Don't bother, I'll catch him myself,' and set off again so that her father had to ease the car into a crawl to stay level. His pedal foot tapped testily. His annoyance rose.

'What do you mean, Maree,' he said, 'are you Jesse Owens all of a sudden? When did you start training for the four-minute mile, Maree? When did you decide you were going to become a track athlete?'

'I want to catch him by myself,' she said angrily. She imagined her father snatching at the horse's broken halter and in doing so scaring it into the path of a truck or bus. Horses were wild, intractable things. Men were brutes. She was thinking how stupid she had been in imagining she could actually have something she wanted. It was not possible, in Maree's family, for a mere girl to attain a dream.

Wishes were horses. That was why they always ran away.

Distracted, Mr Sterry inched the car forward to keep

up. Finally he said, 'Listen, pain-in-the-arse, do you want me to drive you after your silly nag or not? I'll count to three.'

Maree shook her head emphatically and marched.

He shouted, 'Just don't come home without him, girl. That's a 260-dollar stuff-up.'

The blue Ford's oily smoke curled in a stray snatch of wind and spread like wings. Maree remembered a belting she had received from her father after she had called him a sod accidentally, having heard it from her mother's mouth and thought it a term of endearment. *Whump, whump.* Stony gravel skipped out from under each school shoe. She had worn the only leather shoes she possessed; now she wanted to kick them into the dirt, to erase any sense that she had ever been a girl at a school or in a family. She felt alien and savage, Annie Oakley on a suburban street looking for her handsome steed.

'I won't be coming home without him, if that's what you want,' she said dramatically, and there was a long pause.

At last her father made a loud snorting noise, said, 'Suit yourself,' and did a sweeping U-turn, spraying her ankles with gravel like buckshot.

Maree resumed walking. After another block she stopped bothering to look down driveways to see if her horse was there, as children were gathering along the street and as she got closer one or another of them always said, 'He went that way.' Tears kept springing and then drying on her cheeks.

Walking like this, she did not hear Lissa come up behind her until her sister made a broad sweeping arc on her old dragster and said, puffing madly, 'Mum couldn't find the tyre pump, but it was under the sink all the time. How's it going, Ree? Have you seen him yet?'

Maree grunted, 'No.' She was flicking her thigh angrily with the bridle leather. The bit clanged pointlessly. Remembering their earlier fight, she thought that Lissa was merely acting on behalf of her parents and said, 'Why don't you just go home, boy-lover?'

Lissa swished around her in wobbly figure-eights. Perhaps she had not heard Maree's remark; she had something clutched to her stomach and was having trouble trying to steer as well. The bicycle kept foundering past, turning and wobbling back to Maree. Finally Maree stopped in the centre of the road, put her hands on her hips and said, 'What the hell do you want?'

Lissa back-pedalled to a squeaky halt and held out a thermos.

'It's hot chocolate,' she said. 'Mum said it's getting late. Why don't you come home and ring the police? They could send out a car or something, or maybe the RSPCA have a horse catcher who could help.' Her innate good humour made her serene. In the face of her own agitation, Maree despised this serenity most of all.

'Police would probably shoot him,' she said unreasonably. 'I'll find him myself. It's all my fault for having such a stupid little sister and for living with such creeps who I hate, hate, hate!' Her voice rose in a wail, and strangers in houses were tinkling blinds to see.

Lissa sat back on her dragster seat and regarded her younger sister thoughtfully. 'You might at least have a drink, since Mum made it for you,' she said, and coaxingly opened the thermos.

A rich smell of chocolate assailed the air. Maree tried

to skip around the bike but Lissa made a grand show of getting in the way, without spilling a drop.

Finally, to get rid of Lissa, Maree held out her hand. As usual the chocolate was too sweet to drink, and too hot to take more than a sip to coat the tongue. She handed the thermos back.

Lissa said, 'If you frown like that for much longer, you'll get wrinkles and have to have a facelift before you're fourteen.'

Maree said, 'I'm already fourteen.' Lissa tucked the thermos back under her arm. She was too gangly for the dragster, and her knees almost met her chin in trying to pedal on it. She curled around in circles after Maree, crying, 'It's not the point, Maree, you don't understand. How would you like to be Mum, having to put up with Dad all the time?' Her speech grew into a tirade. 'Oh, I think Dad's just on the warpath again, the stupid old mean prick, I mean, who cares what he says anyway, Maree, because we've still got each other.' She made it sound like she and Maree were running away together. 'Anyway, I might not know much about horses, but I can tell that you really wanted that one.' Seeing that Maree was not going to quit walking, Lissa got off the bike and walked alongside, tall and gawky because she had not changed out of her chunky heels, her face taut with concern.

Everything came out in a rush. Maree said, 'I hate it when he calls something I want stupid, but he always, *always* does it. What is he, perfect? He thinks he's a god or something.'

Lissa was nodding. Dingy streamers hung listlessly off the dragster's handlebars, the blue long faded to an even grey. After a while she pushed the handlebars toward Maree and said, 'Here, you can have the bike if you like, so you can go faster. The tyre's getting lower but it'll last a bit longer. I'll go back home and try and keep Mum calm. She started slamming crockery around a little while ago, and Dad's gone to the bottle shop and they're not talking to each other.'

But Maree was stubborn. Her hatred had given her a sort of safety shield; now she felt it dissipating. She thought of Samantha and the shield returned. She said, 'I don't care. I don't want the stupid bike.'

She stood with her hands on her hips, glaring, until Lissa finally gave up. Ever sympathetic, Lissa said, 'Oh, well, hope you find him soon, sis,' and pedalled wobblingly away in the direction of home.

Daylight was waning. There were children everywhere in the gutters, playing with bicycles or toy trucks, waving fairy wands, running tea-parties and giggling at her as she stumbled along. Once, she saw a big grey shape in the front yard of a house, just eclipsed by a red car, and for a moment thought that someone had had the presence of mind to catch the horse and hold it; then she saw that the shape was merely that of a delimbed ghost gum, its dis-membered branches lying on the ground. Maree passed dispiritedly. A man in front of another house waited until she had progressed to the next house along before he called out, 'If you're looking for your horse, he turned left up there.' In the gauzy house shadows behind him, people laughed.

At the end of the street she found fresh dung in a neat heap in the gutter, nosed by a scrawny blue cattle dog with a studded collar. The dog sneezed and ambled away. It was not a part of the suburb she'd often been in, and despite the mangy dog the houses felt posh and unfamiliar. The front lawns were tidy rows of buffalo grass, and in patches around leafy plane trees beside the bitumen, snatches of paspalum and other grasses grew among silky nasturtiums. Near one of these trees the grass had a pulled-at look.

A little boy came running out with a buzzy toy aeroplane and watched her silently for a few seconds, his mouth drooling. Then his older sister came forward as well, a pink-clad frilly girl clutching a doll.

The girl said, 'Um, excuse me, are you looking for a horse?'

Maree nodded in a tired way.

'Well, um, there were some boys here, and they, they were throwing rocks at it, weren't they Scott?'

The little boy nodded vacantly.

Maree said urgently, 'They didn't hit him, did they?'

The girl shook her head, then added, 'I don't know. My Daddy tried to catch him, um, but he ran away.'

'Did he keep going up here or did he turn down that street there?'

'Up there, I think.' The girl pointed vaguely.

Just then a man came out of the house, gave Maree a bored look and said, 'Your horse went back up there.' His finger pointed in the opposite direction to the girl's.

The afternoon was flooded with pink. A car tooted behind her but did not stop. Over its passing she heard a thin whistle and saw familiar craning heads. The pink door rattled conspicuously.

The blue station wagon reached the end of the street and trundled over a low guttering to the entrance of a nature reserve, where it stopped. Heads and arms gestured within and eventually, the car moved into the reserve and parked.

Faces peered whitely at Maree as if wondering what she would do now. She turned toward the houses she had passed, where women and young children were milling about or gesturing in all directions. There was a collective sense of held breaths and gossip; of action plans and curiosity. To these people, she must have seemed other-worldly, a girl from a place where horses were kept or escaped. The straggly crowd was waiting for something to happen.

She swore loudly, like a hooligan. Even now, her pink-doored family had moved into the territory ahead as though prepared to claim it. They were as much a part of her as the brown birthmark above her eyelid and the mole on her right heel. Nothing she could do would remove their thready roots, for they trailed deep into her skin.

Sighing, she put her head down and marched.

Maree's mother, Samantha with a thumb stuck in her mouth, and Lissa were all standing around outside the car, which was parked with its doors akimbo. Maree could not see her father. At the far end of the reserve was a section of tidy mounds planted with bottlebrush trees. Behind that was the rear entrance to a primary school. Walking with magnificent indifference, Maree headed for the bottlebrush.

Lissa shouted, 'She's here, Mum.' She hopped off and marched toward Maree, holding the thermos out again.

Jangling the bridle at her, Maree said, 'I don't want any more. Just leave me alone.'

Her mother, coming around from the car's bonnet, shouted, 'Has she seen the horse yet?' Cigarette smoke clouded above her head.

'I don't know. She won't talk,' Lissa called back.

She dropped behind and Maree kept marching.

Just before she got out of earshot, Maree heard her mother shrilling across the park, 'I'm not putting up with this attitude, do you hear? Your father's furious, I'm furious, and if you just showed a little more gratitude when we tried to help, we wouldn't, we wouldn't . . .' Her voice dissolved, in either tremors or distance. Maree stifled a rude rejoinder and made it with a great sense of relief to the bottlebrush trees.

The horse was not there. Maree walked down the footpath to the school.

For some reason, perhaps for mowing purposes or as a minor thoroughfare for locals, a small gate linking the reserve to the school had been left open. To either side of the school fence, bushes closed off access to nearby homes. When she peered between school buildings to the front fence, she saw that it was closed. For the first time she felt hopeful. Unless there were other pedestrian gates left open, her horse was trapped.

Then came a soft whinny of confirmation. It sounded close, merely tucked away behind one of the school buildings. Maree stumbled forward and closed the steel gate behind her. She began to untangle bit rings from bridle. The rein was broken about six inches from the bit ring, but by knotting the free end through the same ring she was able to produce a reasonable new rein. Although short, it seemed strong enough, as long as nobody lunged for the horse in a Catwoman cape. Then she wound her way around the classrooms looking for the grey.

She had barely rounded the first building when two boys in running shorts passed her by bouncing a basketball between them. Their faces were blown with exertion and youth and their expressions were indolent. At each gesture the ball slammed the asphalt. Even the air around them felt violent. Maree tried to avoid eye contact and focussed on the bridle in her hand.

One boy suddenly shouted, 'Yahoo, ride 'em, Cowgirl!' His companion whistled wolfishly, spinning the basketball as though he were Atlas and it a scaled version of the world.

Maree kept walking, her hands clutching the bridle, her legs stumpy and uncoordinated. She imagined climbing on the horse's bare back and running the boys down, trampling them and their basketball into satisfying deflation. She didn't know why she imagined this. It made her think that this was what her horse had been all along: a vessel for retribution. Was every fantasy similarly imbued?

She rounded the corner of a school building, walking now on asphalt. Her school shoes clattered in a familiar way. She turned left and walked between classrooms, listening for another whinny. Then she skirted a toilet block and came to a dead end. Ahead of her was the edge of the schoolgrounds and a high steel mesh fence separating the school from a neighbouring yard. From the other side of this fence, her horse looked up at her. He neighed.

Maree walked up and down the fence, trying to find an entrance. There was none, and it was growing increasingly dark. The horse was ghostly in the narrowing light, and he wheezed breathily through flared nostrils. The yard seemed to belong to a little weatherboard house, which hulked broodily behind peppercorn trees. At the front of the house was a cul-de-sac with a few parked cars under pale streetlight. A dirt driveway led to a gate between the yard and the street, for the yard itself was fenced back off the road, and the school had a short frontage around the cul-de-sac. The horse must have gone down the alleyway after all, for there was no link to the school. Perhaps he had jumped the fence.

As far as Maree could see in the dimming light, the yard was large but it was rough and badly fenced off from the house. Palings dipped to either side of the vertical and there were many gaps.

She snatched up some new-mown lawn from the front of the schoolyard, held the bridle behind her back and climbed the fence, murmuring, 'Here boy, here boy.' The horse shied at her first approach, but then he dipped his head for the grass and began to nibble. Soft grey lips lifted the mown blades, and inside the great head, jaws worked. At last he lowered his head sufficiently for Maree to slip the reins up and over. This time, because the horse was eating, she managed slyly to supply both bit and grass stalks at exactly the same time, so that he found himself with the jointed metal bar where it should be, inside his mouth. Maree stopped, amazed at her luck, holding the main part of the bridle taut in the air above the animal's head so that the bit would not come out. A few strands of grass hung from his mouth, and the horse paused in his chewing to reflect upon this new situation. Then she managed to fit the headpiece over his ears, clumsily ducking each one through the leather strap, without him even attempting to flee.

Maree pulled his forelock out of the brow-band with trembling fingers. Her heart thumped. She buckled up the cheekstrap that went under his throat and then lifted the reins over his head to lead him. He came willingly, step after gangly step, as though apologetic for having escaped.

In the meantime, Lissa had appeared in the schoolyard behind her. She called out excitedly, 'Mum! She's got him! She's got him!'

Maree shrugged but was pleased, and turned the horse briefly to give her sister a nervous wave. Her mother came up with Samantha in hand, and they stood to the rear of Lissa with dazed expressions.

'Don't let him trample you,' her mother said airily, and then, 'Oh! We'll drive around to the gate! Meet you there! Oh, isn't it good!'

They left Maree to go back to the car, chatting animatedly. Maree checked that the bridle was snug and set out to lead her horse toward the gateway, about thirty metres away.

Then she heard a scratching at the paling fence between paddock and house. A dog began to bark.

The horse coughed.

A man's voice rose from the back of the house, and in the twilight his head appeared above the palings. In a second it was withdrawn and she heard the opening of a small timber gate in the palings.

Before the man could come through, a black lionish shape scrambled into the paddock and leaped in her direction. The horse shied, his massive head lifting her in the air a good ten inches before swinging away. However, the leather did not break again and she still had a hold.

Maree said, 'Hi there!' The dog bayed at her legs, dancing about, while she struggled to keep the horse in hand. Although he pulled, he did not rear again. The dog's massive Rottweiler head lunged at her ankles, withdrew and lunged again, while from inside his throat came a terrifying growl.

The man was sixty-five or seventy. He had a stick and he waved it in the air over his head. He was yelling, 'Get off my property! Get off my land!' At his approach, the dog lunged once more and this time took her jeans in his teeth, as well as a pinch of skin. Maree squealed but hung onto the reins, while the horse did a sort of giant's dance about her.

The man said sternly, 'Let go of that horse!' He was waving the stick in the air as though about to belt her with it.

Near tears, she cried, 'Get the dog away!' She kept trying to kick the dog's head, but at each motion his jaws merely found a new clamp. Eventually the owner took hold of his collar with a meaty fist and pulled the panting animal off her.

The man looked at her levelly.

Maree rubbed her leg. 'This is my horse—thanks for catching him for me.' Her voice souned whiny and fragile.

The man was unimpressed. His fingers on the dog's collar twitched. He said, 'Girly, I don't care what your story is. You're standing on my property, so get off.'

Maree said, 'I'm sorry—but this is my horse.'

'I hear you, girl. And I'll give you to the count of five to get off this property before I let this dog go. I don't care whose horse you say he is or where you got him from!'

The horse stood warily at the end of the reins, almost pulling her arm from its socket. Just then the dog lurched toward her again, and in fright her grip on the reins finally came loose. The horse pulled away a few feet, but before he could trot off, the man had snatched the dangling reins and brutally undone the throat latch. Then he flung the bridle as far as he could toward the roadway.

Her big grey trotted off, hind legs like pistons, and turned at the far fence to survey the dog and two humans. It was now so dark that he was something of a smudge against the backdrop. Every few blinks, the sky dimmed noticeably.

The man let the dog go and it launched at her again, this time jumping to terrorise her arms and wrists. Teeth clicked inches from her pulse.

'Not yet, Blackie!' he called, and the animal held off, growling deep in its throat.

Maree ran backward toward the gate that led to the roadway. The darkened ground made her stumble and she realised she was crying, though not in characteristic sobs. All the same, tears made her vision blurry and she had to keep rubbing them away.

The man waved his stick and shouted after Maree, 'Take your filthy bit of leather with you.'

In the passing gloom, Maree picked up the bridle. This man had it in mind to keep her horse, exactly like a thief. With the words, 'The police'll have something to say about this!' she climbed the front driveway gate, the dog's jaws clicking together just out of reach of her heel. The blue Ford was slowly heading toward the cul-de-sac, parking lights on.

When her mother and her sisters pulled up, she was examining her ankle in the streetlight. On the inside, just below the calf, was a blemish in two parts, exactly like a butterfly. Maree could see no actual blood.

Getting out from behind the wheel, her mother said, 'What's wrong?'

Lissa was saying, 'Where's the horse?'

Maree shushed them both. She couldn't see much in the paddock in the dark, though she could still make out the horse against the far fence. The dog was a black thing circling and barking just inside the gate.

'Mum,' she began, but started crying so wholeheartedly that she couldn't get another word out. Her mother, in great confusion, put a hand on Maree's head and drew her toward her chest, struggling to find something to say. Lissa turned away in embarrassment.

A voice just inside the paddock said, 'You and your

kind can buzz off. If I see her here again I'll get me shotgun.'

Maree's mother gasped out an enraged 'Oh!' Lissa bundled Samantha back into her seat. The dog barked and growled at them.

Quietly, her mother said, 'Are your sure it's your horse, Maree?' She asked this nervously, in fear.

Maree was enraged. This, she thought, was typical. Nobody ever believed what she said. Sniffling and wiping her nose, hating the fact that they'd seen her cry, she said, 'Well, what would you care anyhow?'

Over the dog's barking, the man shouted, 'If I see her here again I'll do me block!'

Maree struggled to see through the gloom and her weepy eyes. Lissa thoughtfully handed her a tissue from the glovebox. The man was heading back toward his house, and the dog remained at the fence, quietened to a low growl of sentry.

Maree's mother wrung her hands. 'Perhaps we should come back tomorrow morning. I don't know that there's much we can do about it now.'

'Get his numberplate,' volunteered Lissa.

Maree scowled at her and said, 'We know where he lives already, Einstein. What'll that accomplish?' She blew her nose and dropped the tissue on the ground. Then she thought for a moment and said, 'What if I wait here while you go get Dad?' Her father was an ideal policeman, who always knew how to enforce rules.

But her mother looked concerned. 'I don't want a daughter of mine hanging around the streets at night. I don't think the horse will go anywhere overnight.'

Lissa curled an arm over Maree's shoulders. The horse snorted from the paddock. Maree could no longer make out any of the animal's shape at all. The lights in the house had come on, spilling through the peppercorns but all this revealed was a shadow.

Maree's mother said, 'Perhaps your father will be feeling more approachable in the morning.'

Lissa gently nudged Maree toward the car. 'Never mind, Maree, we'll come back. We'll get him again.' Sam, bug-eyed in the car, said, 'Mummy, are we going to leave the horst behind?'

Then a chain rattled and Maree looked back to see the man at the gate, caught in a patch of streetlight. He was inserting a padlock through the chain links, at the finish of which he said, 'That should keep you out for a while.' Slapping his hands together, he disappeared once again into the dark paddock.

Maree's feet hurt, her coccyx still ached and she was hungry. The chain defeated her. She allowed herself to be led into the car and belted in by her older sister, who crooned, 'It'll be okay, sis.'

On the way home, her mother kept swivelling in the seat to say, 'Hold still, Samantha!' or to check that nobody was trailing them.

Maree whined, 'Do you think Dad would come back tonight if I ask him nicely?'

When they got home, the lounge room was eerily silent. Their father had gone for a lie down. Despondent, Maree sat at the dinner table kicking her chair rung. Her mother cooked potato cakes and spinach and seemed to be in as fine a mood as was possible, for her.

Throughout dinner, Lissa played a table game of fist-on-fist with Samantha, who giggled over-loudly because of Maree's tendency to glare at her. Maree, suffering the loss of her horse, refused to take in a morsel, despite not having eaten for most of the day. She drew bridles and bit rings on the tablecloth with the tine of her fork and attempted to mind-control Samantha into falling off her chair.

Maree's mother, after slapping food onto the plates, did not even bother to tell Maree she had to eat. She just sat there in a high mind, a flush on both cheeks, and that attitude of listening. After Maree had finished picking at her food, even though she was desperately hungry and aware of her body's interior clamour, her mother set her lips and took the plate away. When Samantha stopped, their mother pointed at her plate and said, 'Eat!'

Maree, bruised to the point of martyrdom, began to wash up.

At that point, the bedroom door at the end of the hall opened and they all went still, as if caught. Maree stared into the sink froth, incapable, for the moment, of movement. Their father had never gone to bed during the day before, except once when he had been suffering a mild form of rheumatic illness. Even on Sundays, watching cricket, if he snoozed at all he slept upright, in his chair.

The man of the house did not look at any of his brood. He went straight to the refrigerator and hunted around in the freezer. Maree was trying to think of how to bring up the horse's situation and ask him to drive her back there; nothing else mattered. But as he passed Maree, he said, 'Given up on the nag, eh daughter?' He was flicking ice from the cube tray into a glass.

Maree started guiltily. 'He's at 64 Rosewood Place, locked in somebody's paddock.'

'What do you mean, 64 Rosewood Place? Who's got him?'

'Some horrible old man.' In the face of her father's

potential for anger, she always felt stupid. Yet so far he had merely sounded curious, perhaps even concerned.

Mrs Sterry watched all faces and kept her hands on the kitchen table, palms down, where Lissa was manicuring her mother's cuticles with an orangewood stick. After a pause, she said, 'She chased him all the way to Rosewood, but this man wouldn't let her take him back.' Speaking made her self-conscious, and she removed her hands from Lissa's ministrations and put them in her lap.

Sighing, Lissa packed up her emery boards and sticks and disappeared up the hall toward the bedroom.

Maree's father was holding up his hand in a gesture of peace. He said mildly, 'So what are you going to do, daughter?'

Maree held her breath. The pink rubber gloves made her hands look enormous, deformed and ineffectual. She pulled them out of the sink in an exaggerated shrug. 'What do any of you care?' she said rudely, looking at her mother, Samantha and her father.

There was a silence of a half-second, and then her father drew himself up. 'When I buy this girl a present in future, no matter what for, somebody take me to get my head read,' he muttered to his wife, and headed for the television set.

Mrs Sterry began to pack up the salt and pepper shakers, as though for their own protection. 'You brought it on yourself, Maree,' she said.

Samantha started to giggle, until Maree flicked her with white suds. Then the brat ran squealing from the room.

THIRTEEN

Maree lay in bed listening to her own breathing. The bedroom air felt stuffy and airless. Under her bed was her school bag, empty, and beside it the bridle. When she was sure everybody was asleep, and had lost count of when the house lights had been extinguished, she rose into a sitting position and waited for Lissa to stir.

Nothing happened. Her eyes sought the ceiling over her head. Car headlights slipped like lightning over the wall and around the cornices, and Maree realised she had been falling asleep. She slid out of bed. She was still wearing jeans below her singlet; she put on the same shirt she had worn that day, which lay crumpled at the end of her bed. Then she paused again, but despite the fancy that the back of her sister's head on the pillow was actually a ghoulish version of her face, she had managed not to wake her.

Maree moved her hand around under the bed and located both bag and bridle. The bit clinked together rather loudly, but Lissa did not stir, so she carefully placed it at the bottom of the bag and muffled it with a T-shirt. She packed in stages, by the light of the occasional passing car, which illuminated her hands in stripes. After a while the desire for sleep disappeared altogether, and she found that she could more easily make out shapes in the room.

When she had finished putting a few essential items of clothing in her school bag, she opened the bedroom door and listened in the absolute dark of the hall for some noise from elsewhere in the house. There was none. Amid creaking floorboards and a great sense of drama, she crept to the kitchen, where she opened cupboards and packed a few slices of bread, two cans of baked beans, an apple, and three carrots from the crisper drawer.

She rummaged as silently as possible among the cutlery and pulled out a fruit knife. By touch rather than sight, she located in another drawer a pair of what felt to be pliers.

Now that she was accustomed to silence, Maree found that the whole house seemed to move, reluctantly and creakily. Guttering tapped against the house. Leaves twitched and brushed windowpanes. Carpet rustled under her feet, as though carrying the news of her intended escape to the skirting boards and walls, and thence to the ceiling and eaves. The whole building appeared to tremble with her intent. Had her father been even partly awake, he would certainly have known that untoward events were about to take place.

Maree went to the hallway leading to the front door, and stood there for a moment smelling the breathy, after-hours scents of the family home; the dust under chairs, soaps and chemicals and the fusty inner soles of shoes.

Just as she put her hand upon the front doorknob, there was an unmistakable sound of movement in the hallway.

Maree took a deep breath and turned to find Lissa. She was a bluish glow in the dark hall, her eyes pale orbs.

The older girl whispered, 'Maree, what are you doing?'

'I'm running away,' Maree said flatly. 'Bye bye.'

'Oh, Maree, no,' Lissa hissed. 'Don't. Dad will help you get the horse tomorrow, I'm sure he will. You just have to, I don't know, be patient.'

Self-pity welled in Maree. 'Dad can get lost,' she said. 'He always ridicules me. He's a pig, a tyrant.' Their whisperings had grown in tone, so that every second she expected her father to stride out saying, 'Running away? What's all this about running away?'

Lissa said gloomily, 'Well, if you won't wait for the morning, wait for me to get my shoes. I'll come too.' Lissa was a veteran of night-time adventures, although never on behalf of a horse. She slipped back up the hall and was gone. Maree was still standing with her hand on the door-knob, trying to decide what to do. If she just left, Lissa would be bound to follow, and Maree did not consider running away to be actually running away if the runner was accompanied. If Maree waited, Lissa would probably convince her to go back into the bedroom and unpack. But this was the first time that Maree, lying awake, managing to stave off sleep, had ever managed to connect impetus with action. It was now or never. She opened the door to the summer air and stepped through. Night floated about, balmy and indifferent. The door closed quietly on Lissa's soft cry. A light breeze carried the taint of cars. Somewhere, a dog howled.

She tiptoed off the porch and began a soft jog in the direction of Rosewood Place. Lissa caught up with her before she was three houses feet down the street. Despite the streetlights, Maree could hardly make out the bitumen upon which she fleetingly placed each foot, and the school bag was ungainly. She was already forced to shuffle to save pitching head-first onto the black tar.

Lissa said, 'I'm not letting you go off alone, Maree. We're in this together.'

They looked at each other in the flickers of light and shade. Lissa's face was a formless oval in the darkness.

'All right,' Maree said, 'you can do whatever you want. But I'm not going home ever again, not unless I get the horse back and Dad apologises and everything changes. For the better.'

'Okay, I won't tell you to go home.' They stopped and stood in the street for a moment, listening to the swish of cars on a major road nearby and glancing over their shoulders into neighbouring front yards and dark spaces. Every now and then a dog set to barking and then all the local dogs followed suit.

They both said at the same time, 'Okay then.'

They started walking.

By night, the suburb was an alien space. Most houses were in darkness, since it was past midnight, but every now and then a home kept its interior burning. Past these houses, Maree developed a runaway's fearful slouch, and even Lissa glanced over her shoulder from time to time. A car, rounding a corner, threatened them with headlights, and Maree took Lissa's arm and hauled her into the shadows of a hedge. Lissa, unconcerned, muttered, 'It's okay, Maree, it's just somebody going past!' But Maree kept imagining her father out looking for them, ready for retribution.

Lissa got up from their crouch and took the lead. Maree followed, ducking like a criminal. What if her father or mother had been awoken by the front door or their footsteps down the path? What if a neighbour had seen them strolling by and recognised them? What if, when they found the horse, he was being guarded by the Rottweiler?

As they walked, Lissa said, 'Where will you go when you get the horse, Maree? Will you go far?'

'Nowhere. Anywhere. I'll stay for a few days at Danielle's.' This was a lie: she was not thinking ahead, even to that sort of possibility. Danielle's mother would immediately ring her own, and she would be back where she started, perhaps with a boxed ear.

But Lissa was also struggling with her school-bred logic. 'What if you bring him back home, Maree, and then decide tomorrow, when it's daylight? Dad's cruel sometimes, or maybe he's just thoughtless, but he means well.'

Maree said, 'Bullshit.'

With a scanty pause, her sister said, 'I guess you might be right.' Lissa was thinking of the trouble she had got into at Maree's age when she once stayed overnight at Andrea's place without asking permission from their parents first. She had rung from Andrea's house at dinnertime, and despite her mother's urgent entreaties and threats refused to come home. That night, her father had driven to Andrea's house and brought her back in tears, grounded for two weeks and with a slapped face. She had lain on her bed saying over and over, 'He's a prick, prick, prick,' while Maree had simply gone about getting ready for school, unconcerned by what she saw then as Lissa's emotional extravagances.

Unexpectedly, Lissa stopped. She said, 'Maree, whose idea do you think it was to buy you the horse?'

'Dad's, but so what? I would have bought one of my own in a few years, when I was old enough.'

'No, it wasn't Dad. I overheard them talking.' She

turned to Maree importantly. 'It wasn't Dad, it was Mum who said they should get you one.'

Maree started, 'What do you mean?'

'Mum was the one who said they should buy you a horse. They were talking in the lounge room. She said since you had your heart so set on it and we weren't doing anything with the side yard except putting rubbish in it he should get you what you wanted. She thought it would make you happy.'

'That's not true!' Maree cried. 'Mum would never think up something like that! And Dad only thought of it because he didn't want to see me getting so skinny.' As an after-thought she said, 'Probably it embarrassed him whenever we went out in public. People thought he didn't feed us enough.'

'I'm only telling you what I heard,' Lissa said breezily, and stopped. 'And what's that not eating thing? They were talking about that, too. So they really were worried, espe-cially Mum.'

They had reached a narrow gateway to a stormwater canal surrounded by grassed embankments, fenced off from neighbouring houses. The canal offered them a short cut. The moon had come out and shone with a cold glow. They were perhaps five minutes' walk from the paddock where the horse was, and half an hour from home when Maree said, 'Why would Mum care about me? She never has before.'

Lissa stood there, scrutinising her younger sister with a look of both pain and sympathy. 'Maree,' she said, 'Mum just wants what's best for you. They both do.'

Maree fisted her hands and let the school bag slump to the ground. 'I didn't ask you to follow,' she said shortly.

'I know you didn't.' Lissa flipped a pebble about in the

toe of her sandshoe. All her motions were posed, like a ballerina. Even removing a stone from her shoe in the moonlight she had her ear cocked for possible spectators, for passers-by. No wonder boys liked her; she existed largely for them.

Irked again, Maree said, 'Well, go home then.'

'No.' She shook her sandshoe and replaced it on her foot, with convincing poise. 'You're not wandering around this time of night by yourself. You might get mugged.'

'You sound just like Mum.'

'I don't care,' Lissa said, 'if I do sound like her. I don't care that you want a horse. I don't even care about the horse. I just want you to be happy.'

The final word echoed off the storm drain walls and dissipated into suburban backyards. It was not the sort of word to echo here. It sounded out of place and time, from some vicinity beyond, books or films. The sisters shivered and looked around. Then Maree picked the bag up and started walking; in a minute she heard footsteps and Lissa caught up.

'Lead on, Macduff. Or is it Macbeth?'

Maree, homework-shy, said, 'I think it's Banquet.'

They marched in step.

The stormwater canal came to an overbridge. They cut up through a dirt footway to emerge on top of it, opposite the cul-de-sac. It was much brighter out here, for the streetlights filled the gaps in the moonlight. The cul-de-sac itself was rather less illuminated, with only one streetlight at the far end, near the school.

Maree grabbed Lissa's arm and they ran across the road. Inside the weatherboard house, a light came on briefly. They were out of sight and earshot, hugging the shadows. When the light was extinguished, they crept the last few metres to the paddock. Maree stared through the darkness, looking for a grey shape to materialise out of the black. Leaving Lissa on the road, she climbed through the fence and began to shuffle in every direction, softly clicking her tongue. She moved cautiously, barely cracking a single twig, and as far as she could tell she did not wake the dog, but all of this made no difference. The horse was not there.

Lissa, waiting on the road, was watching for any sign of life inside the house. When Maree came back, she whispered, 'Did you see him, Ree?'

Maree could not speak for bitterness.

Lissa said, 'Is he not there? Has the man let him go?'

Maree sat down where she was and put her head into her hands to cry. Lissa crouched comfortingly, but her voice sounded relieved. 'We'll have to go back now, Maree,' she said, 'it's the best thing to do. Dad'll come in the morning and find out where he is. Don't run away yet. He's probably around here somewhere, just out of sight, or he's back in the schoolyard or somewhere. The man probably didn't want the police to come.'

Maree was blubbering, 'Oh, the bastard, the bastard,' and Lissa refrained from asking her to whom she referred, her father or the owner of the paddock. Finally she stood up. 'Come on,' she said, 'if we hurry back we'll probably not even have been missed.'

It was nearly one o'clock. Maree stood up in a daze, barely noticing where she put her feet. She began to yawn and realised she was terribly tired. Despite everything, she was glad to be heading home.

When they got there, the house was still in darkness. Lissa said, 'Did you bring a front door key?'

Maree shook her head stupidly.

'We'll have to go around the back.' The back door was

never locked. Lissa brightened up. 'At least they don't look like they've been out looking for us,' she whispered as they clambered through the side yard. Only a neighbour's cat, which had climbed into their yard, made any movement. It leapt deftly over the fence and was gone, leaving Maree to think she had imagined it.

They opened the back door and stood in the entrance to the kitchen, waiting for the lights to be switched on and a booming voice to call them to hell. There was no sound at all but for the echoey tick of the clock in the next room.

Lissa went ahead, holding her running shoes in one hand and tiptoeing exaggeratedly. Maree crept behind her all the way up the hall, until a creaking floorboard once again set her jittery and she hung back to listen. For once she was lucky, as nobody stirred.

Safely in their bedroom, Maree pulled off her clothes and climbed under her sheet. She was so fatigued the ceiling cornices appeared to dive at her like swallows and the gyprock walls to recede and advance mockingly. For the first time she noticed how her heels hung over the end of the mattress, making her tendons ache, while the bed itself dipped in its centre like a hammock and poked at her with springs. Everything in the house was made to order, not to size, bought for cost rather than function. She had outgrown her bed long ago without even realising it; how cramped must Lissa be on the tiny divan? Her sister murmured, 'Night, Ree,' and Maree was rueful enough to whisper, 'Thanks for helping me tonight'. When there was no reply, Lissa already drifting into slumber, she sent her limbs into the corners of her bedding to search for coolness and tried to keep her feet from sticking out. It was useless. Lump-tortured, slung and shifting for better position, she finally curled into an absent foetal and closed her eyes.

FOURTEEN

Despite intending to wake at the earliest flash of dawn, Maree slept in until well after nine. Only Samantha, squealing with laughter out in the lounge room, brought her out of her slumber. She pulled a pair of jeans and a striped T-shirt from her school bag and dressed in these despite the heat, determined to ride her horse at some time during the day. Then she slipped her feet into her school shoes and grabbed the bridle from the bottom of her bag. She stuffed the carrots into her pockets.

In the kitchen, Lissa was putting honey on cornflakes and Sam was running around and around in her plastic cape. She sidled off as Maree approached.

Lissa licked her spoon and put it back into the honey. Last night's escapade was merely a knowing look, which Maree begrudgingly refused to return. She was angry for having slept in, and angry at her sister for not having woken her. Since Maree was angry, Lissa's perennial cheerfulness grated most of all. Her long adolescent arms irritated Maree just by being long. In fact, everything about her family, she reflected, gazing around at the breakfast-table clutter, the discarded papers, the dirty spoons and cups, the food slops on the stovetop, the absence of any order, was somehow integrally wrong.

Maree said, loudly and belligerently, 'When the bloody hell are Mum and Dad getting up, ever?'

Too late she heard her father's tread in the hall, and waited with a sick feeling for him to enter and give her face an irritated backhand. Instead he just walked to the sink to deliver his early morning teacup, wearing a singlet and a dressing gown belted under his paunch. He was in a good mood. He said to the air, 'So Maree's had her beauty sleep now, has she, eh? She's ready to be friends with the world?' As Samantha ran past he lifted her, squealing, into the air.

Maree sat in a moody slump, hating everybody. If her moods were uncontrollable, so was the household. Lissa had given up trying to catch her eye, and took her cereal into the next room to watch TV.

A dull central pain began in Maree's lower stomach. Then the pain passed and at once she wanted to scream or, perhaps, to run at people with a mallet. There was no outlet for this and instead she put her feet up on the chair and curled her arms around her knees and sat there, breathing the cottony scent of her jeans. The bridle, looped carelessly over the chair, pressed into her back.

Her father sat boldly on a chair opposite. After a minute he said, 'Got a problem we don't know about, daughter?'

Maree bit her bottom lip then squeezed it back out from between her teeth, feeling the blood flow again. Her father poured himself a bowl of cereal and hunted briefly for the milk, which was behind a forest of breakfast packets.

Mrs Sterry came into the room wearing a pair of fluffy slippers and her perma-frown.

Maree said, 'Can somebody help me get my horse back, please?'

Maree's father, sprinkling sugar as though he were permitted only a finite number of grains, checking after each spoony wobble, said, 'Why did you let him get anyway, Maree—I mean, moron?'

Maree's mother kicked a pair of shoes out of the way and made for the sink to fill up the kettle. In the lounge room, tinny synthesised music rattled like pebbles in a bucket.

Maree said to her father, 'Because I'm a moron,' and nearly added, 'moron.'

He laughed. 'So I suppose you'd like me to come and help get your horse back, eh? Ask nicely.' He began to eat, the hinge of his jaw grew taut and flexed. It was an infuriating sight.

Maree said, 'If you can get your face out of breakfast.' She had the sudden intuition that she had overshot a border, stepped off a gangway. Below that gangway raged the usual current of paternal retribution. Her father reared himself up.

He took his cereal bowl from the table, tipped it, corn-flakes and all, into the sink, shrugged curtly past her mother, who was busy staring out over the backyard, and headed into the lounge room. On the way he said over his shoulder, 'I will go and see to the bloody horse when I am in the mood to see to the bloody horse, or when that little bitch of a daughter gets a civil tongue!'

The television was curtly flipped to a sports program.

Lissa came out with a 'told you so' look and went off up the hall, cereal bowl in hand.

Their mother, running a hand through her hair, said to Samantha, 'Did you have your breakfast yet?'

Maree grabbed the bridle and marched out the back. The bicycle was propped against the laundry wall. Its rear tyre was flat. She pumped it up again, tested it, and wheeled the bike out the front through the side yard. Her mother watched through the kitchen window, her face devoid of expression as she continued doing whatever she was doing at the sink.

By the time Maree got to the front of the house, the tyre was flat again. She pumped it so hard her arms hurt. Her mother came to stand on the verandah, arms folded and face impassive. Maree climbed on the bike. The rim made a tinny noise as it struck a bump, and rubber squelched as she pedalled away. Her mother called out, 'Maree, aren't you waiting for your father?'

Maree yelled, 'Why should I?'

'Hang on,' her mother said, flapping her arms, 'wait till I get that bloody man!' She went inside, walking like a chicken.

Maree straddled the bike for perhaps half a minute, but only Lissa peered through the venetians and gave her a V for victory sign. Samantha came to the front doorway and began calling Maree's name in a voice that might have been innocently cute or might have been sarcastic. In a burst of fury, Maree pulled a carrot out of her pocket and threw it right at her sister. It hit the door frame inches from the girl's head, and Samantha withdrew with a squeal.

Maree pedalled down the street, following last night's path. There was a stubborn ache in her lower back that every bump on the wheel rim aggravated. At Olympic Way the chain came off, and she walked the rest of the distance with the bike beside her and the bridle intermittently tangling in her legs. The sun was vicious and made her face sweat. She was so tired she used the bicycle to keep her upright rather than the reverse.

When she got to the cul-de-sac, she leaned the bike against the school's fence and walked the few steps to the man's paddock. The grey was not inside it. She walked back and forth along the front fence, peering up the drive-way. At that moment a high, shrill neigh rose from behind the house.

The dog came into the front yard, snuffing at some long grass. He had not noticed her yet. Maree kept very still. When the animal had nosed back around the house, she moved right up to the driveway gate and squinted down the side of the house. At the back of it, in the far reach of her vision, she caught the swish of something that must have been a tail.

He had been put in the houseyard overnight.

At that moment, there was the noise of a truck from the street behind and a ratty old livestock carrier manoeuvred its bulk into the cul-de-sac. Maree stared at it vacantly until, barely a few feet from her, it stopped. A man of an age somewhere between eighteen and twenty-eight climbed down from the cab, glanced at her curiously and went around the back to open the tailgate, which formed a strutted ramp. To Maree he said, 'The old guy out o' bed yet?'

'What?'

By now the black dog had come out and was barking furiously. The truck driver inclined his head toward the fence and raised his eyebrows. His face was freckled and his chin sharp, and he reminded her of the coward in a Western. She disliked him instantly. 'Bed,' he said amicably, 'y' know, that thing yer sleep in.' He mimed sleep, with his head on the side and his hands steepled.

Maree said, 'I don't know what you mean.'

He looked at her quizzically and, hands in his pockets, sauntered over to the gate. Before he got to it, a familiar white head emerged from the rear of the house. It was the man from yesterday. Trotting beside him, led by a piece of rope, came the big skinny grey.

'About time,' the man began confidently, then he saw Maree and his flaccid jaw dropped.

'It's that girl again,' he said. The dog, hearing his tone, starting jumping up and barking again, and Maree was mortally afraid he was going to clamber over the gate and attack her.

The truck driver said, 'She's wanted, is she?' and looked at her.

Maree tried to stand taller, to approach the truck driver in height. He was closer to her age than to the old man's, and something made her believe this would cause him to empathise with her. She said, 'I just wanted to get my horse back. He ran away yesterday.' By way of emphasis she jangled the bridle at them both, showing the broken part.

The cowboy looked blank. Before he could reply, the old man cuffed his dog to shut him up and said, 'Let me tell you, this girl is in for the chop. I'm about ready to shoot her if she tries one more time to pinch my horse.'

Maree said, 'Why would I come back now if I was trying to steal him?'

The truck driver said, 'Sheesh.' He scratched his head. 'Little girl,' he added after a while, 'you don't just walk up and say a horse is yours.'

'I know exactly what my horse is like,' Maree asserted. 'I picked him out, didn't I? And I can prove it. My father's got the receipt. We bought him from a guy at a ranch, I forget the name of the place. Yesterday I chased him this far. When I got here, that man said he didn't care whose horse it was, he just didn't want anybody else on his property. What's that if it's not an admission?'

'You annoying brat!' the old man shouted, growing red in the face. 'Get out of here before I call the police! G'wan!' When he waved his arm the big horse shied backward. The dog began to bark again.

The truck driver said, 'I didn't come here to fight over a nag. I'm just doing me job, eh?' Then he opened the gate, and, after a short hesitation, the man led the horse out. The grey moved nervously, hind legs clopping in an anxious high-step. The cords in his wiry neck stood out thickly as he pranced.

'Out of the way, girl,' the truck driver said, but this time he sounded amused rather than anxious.

Maree said, 'This is stealing, as sure as if you broke into our house.' Waving airily at her, the old man led her horse up the truck ramp. He had closed the gate to bar the dog, but the black beast, Maree saw, was getting his muzzle into a gap. She began dancing about behind the men, crying, 'Thieves! Thieves!' The horse was toey, and skittered one way and another until the truck driver managed to get behind and whee him up with a slap of a stick. Then the skinny beast staggered into the cage and was locked in. His ewe neck was wirier than ever; his soft grey muzzle sniffed the air. His enormous wither rose above the cage top like the crest of a roller-coaster. He whinnied once or twice.

Ignoring Maree, the truck driver and old man saluted each other. Then the former nodded amusedly—or apologetically, she wasn't sure—at Maree and got into the truck.

She cast about for stones or sticks to throw, or something sharp to wedge into the tyre. Then the black dog got the gate open and rushed out and, caution redirected, Maree was suddenly running at the truck sides yelling, 'Help!' The truck was in gear and rumbling, moving slowly down the road, when the dog made a great leap for her buttocks and grabbed at a piece of her. Actually, all he had was a mouthful of bridle. She let go of it. At the same time, she grabbed hold of the wooden slats at the back of the truck and hauled herself up. The dog backed away, snavelling at the old leather and steel.

The man ran along waving his stick, ancient legs almost buckling underneath him. 'Oi there!' he called to the truck driver. 'Just you keep driving.' To Maree he shouted, 'Get off at once, you pest!'

The driver glanced into his rear-view mirror but, not seeing her clinging to his truck, put his foot down. He was already moving too quickly for her to alight, and picking up speed. The horse neighed across the rooftops and shifted, causing the truck to creak. Maree was attached, limpetlike and prayerful, to the wooden boards, too fearful at first to even open her eyes. When she did, she saw that they were about to turn a corner, and taking advantage of the truck's braking she made a Herculean climb over the rails and landed, winded, right at the feet of her horse. He collected himself, sinewy muscles bunching at haunch and shoulder, but just then the truck went round the corner and he shifted all his weight onto his off-side legs. Staggering for traction, he concentrated on remaining upright.

Crouching so she would not be seen, she said softly, 'Hello, horsey horse.' He turned his head in the brief arc that his lead rope made possible, and studied her from one dark-rimmed eye. She was a little frightened at first that he would trample her, but when he did not do so she crept to the rear of the truck's cabin and, buffeted a little from the wind that curled around the cab through the wooden slats, braced herself. She squatted down to keep well clear of the window at the back of the cabin, out of sight of the driver.

About two blocks on, and driving in the direction of her home, the truck was breezing along at a steady rate. They had just passed the turn-off that would have taken her home when she saw the familiar blue car with the pink door pull out, heading in the direction of Rosewood Place. Maree's father was at the wheel, looking distractedly the other way. There was no point in bothering to shout.

They drove, stopping and starting for perhaps half an hour. Maree was badly carsick. Her legs grew tired from crouching, and her watch had stopped. She thought, a little optimistically, that her father might manage to get the old man to tell him where the horse had been sent. Perhaps the animal was being moved to somewhere more secret; she had no idea at all how horse-thieves worked. While wondering, she tried to keep out of the line of sight of following cars. Maree did not want them to flag the driver down until they reached their final destination. Then, she thought, she could telephone home.

The tailboard rattled as though it would fall off. Maree lurched this way and that, and nausea kept her from taking much notice of where they were going. From the truck floorboards came the scent of pig or chicken shit. To keep the sickness at bay, she tried talking to the horse. He shifted slightly so that he was roughly diagonal across the truck. Every now and then he turned his muzzle as far as the halter would strain to check that she had not moved or done anything to threaten him. After a while, he seemed to forget she was there.

They finally slowed and lurched into the rutted driveway of a ramshackle car park. The truck parked alongside a sign that read 'Stock entrance'.

Maree heard the driver whistling as he came around to unbolt the tailgate; it was only when he had walked up the ramp and was undoing the horse's tether that he saw Maree, standing on the other side of the animal. For a moment, his blank cowboy's face registered shock.

'How'd you get in there?' he said.

She smiled wryly because he barely seemed angry, only surprised. Her father would have been furious. 'I climbed,' she said smartly.

Perplexed, he said, 'Lady, I don't like to say get off me truck, but if I'd have seen you before, I'd have chucked you off as quick as said it.' Crease-browed, he looked even more like a cowboy than before.

Maree dusted her jeans with both hands and said, 'Like all thieves.' Then, in an attempt to stall him as he continued untying the horse, 'Where are we, the abattoir?' She was terrified that her horse was going to be killed. 'You wouldn't want to take him in there if you want to stay out of gaol,' she said feverishly.

The cowboy said, 'Where'd you spring from, kid? You're a laugh and a half.'

She said, 'Where'd you spring from, the gaol?'

He moved the horse backward, almost trampling her, and said, 'You reckon Winterson's a liar, eh?'

Ducking under the lead rope, Maree climbed down ahead of them; he was backing the horse out, pushing at the shoulder. Too late she thought of putting the ramp back up, but she probably could not have lifted it anyway. There was nothing she could do to delay him except be obnoxious, so again she danced around the man and the horse, demanding them to stop.

He laughed until Maree shut up. She sidled beside the open ramp until she was level with him and said, 'Maybe this Winterson guy lost his own grey horse and he really thinks this one is his. It could happen.'

The driver clicked his tongue. The horse backed further down the ramp, his clumsy great hooves slipping onto each cross-strut, and at the final half-metre one of his hooves came off the ramp altogether. The animal nearly fell. When he had righted himself and was safely at ground level, the driver squinted at her and scratched his upper lip.

'Tell you what,' he said. 'If you can get proof of what you're saying, I'll make sure whoever buys 'im knows who to call. That's the best I can do.'

Maree said, ' "Who buys him"? You can't. He's not for sale.'

The driver patted the horse's gaunt neck. 'He has to be, kid. It's what we come for, ain't it?'

Maree's horse kept lipping at the driver's hand, ducking his jaw back against the tug, eager to move at each manoeuvre of the lead rope. She glanced wildly about for a phone booth or an office, but the area was full of old trucks and cars and the only buildings nearby seemed to be inside the gates of the auction yard. Across the road were only a closed-looking lawnmower shop and a stretch of vacant blocks behind a shabby bitumen footpath.

The truck driver led the horse toward the entrance, casually flicking him behind the girth with the tail end of the lead rope. Maree followed, biting at the inside of her cheek. Nothing she wished for ever turned out. Simple desires were always thwarted into tagging along at some-body else's behest.

As she walked, the horse released wind hissily and methane drifted at her in noxious clouds.

A burly, hunched man sat on an upright log at the entrance to the yards. He waved a clipboard at the driver and said, 'G'day, Kenneth.' When the driver saluted, he made a tick on his clipboard pad and grinned him through.

Maree's horse lowered his head and sniffed the earth. Kenneth jerked the rope, clicked his tongue, and the skinny, flecked horse shied as he stumbled through the gateway.

Maree went up to the man with the clipboard. 'Excuse me,' she said, and had to say it two or three times before he would look up.

'What is it, girlie?' he said with a fatherly smile.

'That man, the one who took that horse. What's his name?'

'You don't know him? That's the famous Kenneth.' He chuckled as though she ought to have heard of him.

'He's got my horse.'

'What, you're selling him?'

'No, it was a mistake, he's bringing him here for some-one else who stole him. But it's my horse and I want to stop him.'

The steward frowned. He took an old fob-watch out of a pocket in his white coat and said, standing a little straighter, 'Well, now that sounds like a difficult situation, see, 'cause I just enter the stock on the auction book here, and at the moment I'm supposed to be closing the lots so we can start proceedings. I'm not the man strictly in the know, see?'

'Well, can't you take that last horse off the list? I don't want you to sell him. He's a stolen horse.'

He stared at her as though she'd blasphemed. 'I don't know as I can remove an entry just on your say so,' he said, 'unless your name is,' and he read from the clipboard, 'G. H. Winterson.'

Maree thought of pretending she was, but had a sudden intuition that the steward knew exactly to whom the initials referred.

'Please,' she said, 'can you tell me where I can find a phone? All I have to do is let my parents know, and they'll be here with proof.'

The steward patted his pockets without apparent purpose. He stretched out one knee arthritically and stood up. Both the truck driver and her horse had disappeared. The man shuffled through the entranceway, drawing the gate closed after them, affecting a prim air. Then he turned and said, 'Tell you what, darlin', it's Benjamin Stow, the auctioneer you want. He'll show you the office. He organises things round here. He's what you might call a great all-rounder.' The steward laughed wheezily.

Maree said, 'Benjamin Stow?'

'BJ, Benjamin Stow. He's the guy with the gavel. You'll find him in the tent, they're up to tack, I should think.' He smiled pleasantly and turned to chain the gate.

Maree ran though a moleskinned, flannelletted crowd, looking dizzily this way and that in an effort to spot her horse so that she would be able to point him out. For all she knew the driver might have hidden him somewhere or put him straight onto the back of another truck. There were women with overdone hair and sharply comparative eyes in the company of such heavy-set men. Maree felt that her own hair had taken wings, so far did it stick out from her head. Over-the-hill cowboys with their bootheels up on timber rungs ignored her completely as she rushed around.

At every turn she expected boys of the type she went to school with to shout, 'On ya, slut!'

She roved the marketplace as though in a daze. She could not locate horse or driver, but she did find the autioneer's tent. Inside, the tent smelled of furniture polish and neat's-foot oil. Great draperies of tack covered long trestle tables and makeshift masonite stands, marked with lot numbers in the three-to-five hundreds. The bulk of it looked like torture devices, with the exception of number 486. That was a cage full of rabbits, among a table strewn with stirrup irons, silver forks, hoof-trimming implements and bitless bridles.

Perhaps the rabbits were to be tortured.

Maree reached a crowded section where she had to shoulder through, desperately hoping that the auction had not yet begun. She could sense rather than see a figure on a stand of crates.

But the auction was indeed underway and the sonorous voice of the auctioneer rose into the tent's space, all the garbled syllables of it, consonants running together and vowels in a whirr like an amazing warbling bird reciting numbers.

'Eighty bid, eighty bid, eighty bid, we have eighty bid, do we have eighty-five, eighty-five bid, eighty-five bid, that's eighty-five bid, do we have ninety, yes we have ninety, we have ninety, do we have an advance on ninety, any advance on ninety, ninety is as ninety does, ninety going once, ninety going twice, ninety going three times. Ninety all? Ninety all?' There was a loud whack. 'Sold to the man in the far corner there at ninety bid, give 'im a ticket, Lou.'

Around Maree, people shuffled and craned, each perhaps with a heart set on a particular item hours down the list. Maree knew that she had no hope of getting to speak to the auctioneer, and nobody else around seemed to have any part in the running of things, but for a chickenlike man who flitted here and there holding items up for view and passing successful purchasers their little green slips of ownership and obligation to pay.

Outside in fresher air, she came upon a group of enormous-hatted men with their bootheels up on a corral fence, and she said in desperation, 'Excuse me, I'm looking for somebody called Ken.'

They laughed. Then one leaned back and said, 'Not Cootamundra Ken?'

A second man, spitting a tiny amount of beer back into his can, said, 'Nah, mate, she wouldn't want Cootamundra Ken. No gal in her right mind'd want Cootamundra Ken.'

There were raucous laughs. Maree waited in agonised mock-politeness. There was some discussion about Cootamundra Ken, terminating in the statement 'He's gone up north.' The men all took a religious swig of beer and seemed to forget Maree's initial question in their sudden solemnity.

She said, 'I don't know his full name. The steward at the front said he was called the famous Kenneth.' In her lame voice this sounded stupid. These men were horse and cow men; they probably never noticed who else trooped through the auctions or rodeos, and they probably never usually bothered to speak to teenage girls. But they put their heads together in a serious fashion and she heard one say, 'Maybe she's talking about Ken the saddler,' and another say, 'No, he's long gone, he's in Darwin.' The man furthest away pioneered, 'What about dog Ken?'

There was a brief stillness, then they all seemed to agree it was probably dog Ken.

Maree said, 'Where could I find him?'

'Over that way,' they said straight-faced, 'with the dogs.' Patiently, they pointed to another tent.

Maree thanked them and left them to their boot-up yarning. She forgot to ask them about a phone and, a few steps away, decided not to bother going through the ritual a second time.

In the smaller tent it was so dark that she was hit with a waft of chicken manure before she could see anything. Walls of chicken cages came to vision as her eyes adjusted, hundreds upon hundreds of birds pressed in upon one another and reaching from floor to ceiling, scattering the air with feathers and a heavy, chooky smell. Maree wandered a little further in, but this tent appeared to have no people and she had the thought that the men had pointed her toward the wrong Ken after all. Yet she didn't want him, she just wanted to see where the horse had been put.

She found a man fitting a latch onto a cage at the far end of the tent, in which, amid all the chickens, he had placed a trio of cross-bred puppies. 'After a pet, lovie?' he asked when she couldn't help stooping to poke a finger in the cage.

She said, 'No, thanks anyway.' She was about to go, but had one last try. 'I'm looking for somebody called Ken, walking around with a big grey horse.'

The man stood up creakily, looking little and misshapen under an enormous woollen vest. White pants had gone brown on their thighs from years, she guessed, of wiping sweaty hands. He pointed out through a side exit, toward a slightly downhill row of farming implements. At the bottom, she could see a maze of wooden corrals and, finally, a paddock in which horses grazed, just visible between the piles of junk and trooping customers in jeans and riding boots. The place was a maze; it would have taken her much absent wandering to find even the horses.

'Try down there, if it's young Ken you want.'

Maree mumbled thanks, and ran.

Had she not been on a mission, she might have paused to watch the auction-goers as they meandered past every conceivable type of farm and domestic implement. People seemed spellbound by old or rusted objects; she glimpsed two men musing over an ancient rotary hoe, and a woman scribbling ineffectively at years of green grime in a claw-toed bathtub. Infants in strollers pointed at strange objects and cried to be taken closer and allowed to clutch. Giant springs were allotted white tags as though they, too, would find in this makeshift camp a new home and purpose. Endless rusted coils of wire, barbed, meshed and single-stranded, waited in corners to be unfurled into the boundaries on newly subdivided farms.

At the bottom of the hill she found the horses, which were being kept in a large timber holding yard. There were forty or fifty animals of varying shapes and sizes, from emaciated yearlings with scatty, wormy-looking hides to old brood mares and even some youthful, if bony, hacks and hunter types. Drinking from a trough, face flecked with manure from other horses' kicks, was her elusive, lanky grey.

He looked utterly at home among the nondescript herd.

Maree climbed through the corral fence, clicking her tongue. The horse blinked back at her and did not flinch as she approached. She put her arms around his neck, wishing for a rope or piece of strap to hold him with, and cursing the Rottweiler for removing the one essential item of tack from her person. Familiar with holding yards, and perhaps only safe to ride or handle while enclosed, the animal dipped his muzzle to her shirt and snuffed gently. Then he shook his head and blew heartily through quivering nostrils, spattering her with lime.

Pleased at this gesture of acknowledgement, she wiped her forearm across her hip.

Other ponies and horses milled around a wispy scattering of windblown chaff, or pulled fragments of lucerne from the churned earth with their nimble lips. Straggling buyers came to the corral and ducked through the timbers to inspect the mouths of various animals. A hefty, clean-dressed man of about forty gave her a nod in passing, and on his way back said, 'He's big for a pacer. What is he, six year old?'

Maree said, 'He's not for sale,' and the man gave her a queer look.

He said, 'Better get him out of the holding pen, then. Auction won't be long.'

Now that she had found the grey she was reluctant to leave. The moment she actually rang her parents to tell them, the real trouble would begin. She would have to explain how she got to the sale yard, for instance, and Maree knew that there would be no excuse in her parents' repertoire of excuses for a girl climbing onto the truck of a strange man. She had seen Lissa's face slapped for far less than that. And there was the issue, once she did find a telephone and make the call, of whether they would actually help.

But a girl alone in the world was even more doomed than a girl with a family. She kept a wary eye out for Ken in case he had other plans for her horse, and went to where a steward was minding a gate.

'Excuse me,' she said, 'What suburb is this?'

He gave her a sleepy glance. 'You mean town.'

'Town, then.'

'Or village.' He peered at her boredly, already sick of joking at her expense. 'It's Naraville.'

'Where's Naraville?'

'Well, some'd say it's the middle of Narawhere.'

She ignored that. 'All right. And this is the Naraville auction, I suppose?'

'Clever girl.' He yawned.

Dislike for him made her nostrils clench. 'Could I also ask, is there a phone nearby? My horse was stolen this morning and he's been put in the yard there so I really ought to be calling the police.' Her voice was high and affected. In the face of obstinacy she was morbidly polite.

The man was rubbing his greasy fingernails up and down the front of his checkered shirt, where there was a button missing. A surprisingly white singlet peered out. 'Lady,' he said, 'I don't know if you should go round making allegations. What do you mean somebody stole your horse?' All the same, he seemed serious.

She said, 'Somebody called Ken. Kenneth.'

'Kenneth who?'

'I don't know. He was working for Mr Winterson.'

'What, old Graham? That Winterson?' His posture softened. 'Y' can't mean him. He's been bringing horses here longer than I was born.' As though to demonstrate the truth of this, his eye slid to her breast.

She crossed her arms. 'The horse was stolen from me this morning. The Ken I mean has a red truck, sort of a cattle truck, with a big door.' She mimed the door in the air. 'He didn't realise the horse was mine, if it's any help.' This, she felt, was doing the driver a favour, but the steward began to slap his knees and laugh.

'Do you know who you're talking about, girl?' he

asked, doubled over. Then a movement in the crowd caught his eye and he righted himself to call out across the dusty walkway, 'Hey, Vasty, you know anything about some horse Graham Winterson's got up for sale? Here with trucky Ken?'

Vasty was a smallish boy, perhaps not quite Maree's age, but what made him alien to her was beyond age or physique, it was upbringing. Or gender. He was folding a rope halter over and over and had a narky, brooding expression. He looked Maree up and down like a butcher a skinny cow.

'Who wants to know?' he asked.

The steward pointed with a chapped thumb.

The boy said, 'So?'

'She says it's pinched.'

The kid shrugged. 'I gotta find a frigging lead rope,' he said, 'I've got plenty to worry about with that appy piece of shit.' Then he sauntered away.

The steward looked at Maree and shrugged. He seemed, fleetingly, apologetic. 'You could try the service station across the road for a phone.'

She said, 'It really is my horse. When my parents turn up they'll bring the receipt.'

He nodded and appeared not to listen. Then, when she was about to walk away, he said, 'BJ's the one you want to impress, kiddo. He's the guy in charge round here. He'll halt the sale if there's been any impropriety.'

When she had moved off, she heard a shout of 'Lady! Lady with the pinched horse!' and looked around. The steward was beckoning to her with a fat finger.

'Who'd you say the horse you're looking for come with?'

Scowling, she kicked the dirt. 'Somebody called Ken,

young Ken. About this tall, wearing a sort of red-checked shirt, freckles, blond curly hair.'

He closed his eyes again and rubbed his back against the corral once more to relieve some ancient itch. Finally he looked right above her head and said, 'Gal here's got a word to say about you, Ken.'

Maree turned. The driver she had been hunting for was ambling right past, eating a Pluto Pup.

'Oh, the pest again.' He winked to the steward and made as though to keep walking.

Maree walked up to him and tugged his sleeve, causing the steward to double over in laughter. 'The police are on their way. I'm just waiting for them to get here. They said they'll take, oh, fifteen minutes and then you better have a story ready.'

Instantly, the truck driver halted, the snack up to his face. Maree crossed her arms, and stared at him. Her face felt hot. She sensed the implausibility of winning him over to her side even as she decided to have a go at it.

'Yesterday,' she said as he took another bite, 'the grey horse that you've brought here in your truck was near our front yard, where I was holding him and trying to lead him to some grass. Then my sister scared him and he ran away. I followed him all the way to that old man's house, where he was this morning when you picked him up. Today he's here. You brought him. All I'm trying to do is get my horse back.' Tears came to the corners of her eyes.

Ken leaned against the gate and looked for a juicy part of his sausage-and-sauce monstrosity to cram into his face. Despite the situation, despite her hatred of all things meaty and sauced, Maree's mouth watered.

She went on, 'When I was leading him out of our side yard, my sister leapt at him and he bolted. Now he's in a yard with a hundred other horses and you don't care if he gets sold or not, because it's just not your concern, is it?'

Ken nodded a greeting over her head at somebody, mouth too full to talk. But he looked at her as though to keep her speaking.

'So that's it,' she wailed, 'you are stealing him. You and Mr Winterson.' Even to her, her voice sounded strained, far-fetched.

The driver cleared his mouth and said, 'You didn't have any proof he was yours, and I've got nothin' against Winterson. Why didn't you bring a receipt or a photo or something?'

'I didn't have a photo, there wasn't time. I only had him for half a day.'

Ken nodded understandingly and she realised he was having a joke at her expense, pretending to be serious. His sharp chin wore a trickle of sauce. In desperation, she said, 'The stupid bastard with the paddock wouldn't let me any closer to have a good look in daylight. He was too busy trying to sell the evidence.'

Ken said, taking another bite, 'That "stupid bastard" has bred his share of horses in his time. You telling me he basically stole your horse? Well, that's a pretty mean accusation.'

'I don't care,' she whined, 'I'm not going to send him to gaol or anything. If he cooperates now he won't get into trouble, I'll see to that.'

Her claim amused the cowboy. 'This guy has had horses twenty, thirty years,' he said, wiping a hand on his mole-skins. 'How long you been riding, you wanna tell me?'

'Plenty,' Maree said. He didn't seem convinced. Still he munched away, down to the stick, which he stripped casually by sliding it between his teeth. There was a certain horrible joy in watching him eat; it was like watching a leopard devouring part of a cow's hindquarter. He threw the stick against a railing and it ricocheted into a bin.

'You beauty,' he said, and wiped his hands again on his dirty moleskins. He looked at her appraisingly and picked at his teeth with the back of a finger, making little sucky noises.

Maree wondered whether BJ What's-his-name was up to the horses yet. But Ken was still picking his teeth, in no hurry to move. She had to find a phone.

She asked tetchily, 'Have they already finished with the other stuff?'

'Nah,' he said evenly. 'They usually do the pricey things first, show saddles and complete outfits. Next they'll do a couple tractors they got parked up the side, and some other heavy equipment, then, ah, the chickens and shit. Nags aren't till the afternoon.' She suddenly had the sense that he was studying her, and turned away self-consciously. 'You never been to an auction before?' he asked.

She said she hadn't.

'How old are you?'

Her stomach flipped oddly. She answered, 'Sixteen,' a lie by eighteen months.

He nodded in a way that implied a glimmer of satisfaction, and she suddenly wondered why she had chosen that age rather than seventeen, which sounded less obvious, less legally marked.

Predictably, he said, 'Old enough, eh?'

She said, 'Do you get a kick out of stealing girls' horses, whatever age they are?'

He picked his teeth at something lodged and tenacious. 'You're no way sixteen,' he said, 'though I'd say, considerin' how developed you are, fifteen and a half.'

'I know my own horse,' she persisted, 'even if I did only have him for an hour.' Meaning to invite pity, she realised as she spoke how stupid that made her sound.

Ken slapped his thigh. 'Well,' he said, 'she knows her horse, but does her horse know her?'

As though he'd made a great witticism he clutched at his knees and doubled over, gasping. After a minute she realised he was choking. Maree stood there looking on with a vague sort of disapproval, half hoping he would choke to death. When he had stopped spluttering he stood up straight and spat a copious cowboy's spit onto a timber ledge, where it clung briefly. He finally said, 'Guess you could say things like that just stick in me craw.'

Appalled, she started walking off.

He made an apologetic sound.

Maree turned around and said, 'What?' coldly.

'I lied,' he confessed glibly, and she saw the row of striding auction-goers, all marching toward the main corral. The driver laughed uproariously at his own joke. 'They do the horses now, little Miss Sixteen, not after the old farm junk. So why don't you go and make a bid if you like the old grey so much?'

FIFTEEN

Maree ran into and through the crowd, elbowing for space and direction. She was so furious she kept inventing revenge schemes, including letting the truck tyres down, only she was terrified of getting caught. If she had known how to drive (which foot was the brake?) she would have gone back and tried to pick the cowboy's pocket for his keys. Every few seconds, she would find somebody who looked to be slouching knowingly, and say, 'Excuse me, do you know where I could find a phone?' Everybody either shrugged, said, 'No, sorry,' or pointed vaguely to a far tent at the top of the auction yard where they said there was an office.

Maree never found the office. It did not actually exist, so far as she was able to work out, for B.J. Stow was a sort of mobile office himself, and the chicken-man his ambulatory secretary. Finally, a calm-faced woman looking through a box of assorted rusty bits said, 'There's a service station over the road, sweetheart. Why don't you try there?' She seemed so kind compared to everybody else that Maree almost collapsed in gratitude.

She jogged through the entrance and emerged in the parking lot. 'Over the road' turned out to be about four blocks' worth of empty street down the hill, and one block up another street. She found the petrol station and had to harass the proprietor to let her use his office phone, as the red one at the front was out of order. An ox of a man with bright orange hair and myriad tattoos of women with their breasts exposed, he hovered by Maree, jangling his keys while she dialled and asked for reverse charges, betting all hopes on the fact that Lissa would answer the phone and accept.

If she had had any money at all, she would have rung the police, but she did not have a cent on her.

The phone was answered by Samantha, who said, 'What? What?' until the phone was wrested from her by Lissa.

When Lissa had approved the charge, Maree said, 'Is Dad there?'

Lissa sounded frantic. 'Where are you? Mum and Dad are looking for you everywhere. I told you not to run away, Maree, I told you to wait for Dad.'

'I'm at something called Naraville Auction. Where are they looking for me? They don't know where I am.' Climbing onto the back of the truck had seemed the only course of action at the time.

Lissa was saying, 'Oh, they went to the school, they went to Danielle's, they drove up and down the streets looking out for you or that stupid horse. They're really angry, Maree, I've never seen them this angry.'

The ox-man behind her cleared his throat and almost, she thought, went to grab the receiver to cut her off. He was impatient to get her out of his office. She said quickly, 'Will you tell Mum or Dad I'm at an auction? They're trying to sell the horse. If they care at all, they could come here now and bring some proof and then we'd have both the horse and me back, okay? I wouldn't care what trouble I was in. And if they don't come to pick me up, then I don't even know if I'll make it home at all. There are some pretty weird people here.'

Lissa said, 'Well, if I were you I'd forget the horse and come back home, on the double. Dad's so angry he broke the recliner lever.' She started to laugh a little hysterically, and in the background Samantha was squealing.

'Well, tell Mum and Dad I'm not coming home without the horse.'

She hung up on her sister's sorrowful 'Oh Maree!'

The orange-haired man gave her a stern look, and appeared about to give some advice, but she ran off. By the time she returned to the saleyards, she was out of breath and the auction of horses had begun.

For a few minutes, elbowing her way through the crowd, she thought the grey had already been dealt with. Then she realised that her horse was still inside the holding yard, even though many of the other horses had been moved for a final grooming. His hind leg rested on its toe-tip, and his ears were continuously swivelling to follow the faraway noise. He looked calm, and for the time being there was nobody at the gate. Maree did not have a rope of any kind, or she might have led him right out.

She went back to the central corral where the crowd had mustered. She had no hope at all now; she could only watch the horses come through and take note of the outcome. The auctioneer was shuffling around getting comfortable in a tiny booth above the ring. Somebody was organising the first few horses into a sort of chute. It had a lot in common with a rodeo.

Almost by accident she found Ken, standing among a gang of slouchers, Akubras pulled down in varying degrees over their eyes and drinking beer in gold ring-pull cans. He had his boots up on an esky. Maree had considered as a last resort speaking to the auctioneer or somebody else in charge, but on seeing the enemy she changed her mind.

She said sullenly, 'I'm after him,' pointing with a cowboyish nod rather than with her finger to Ken at the far end. The men nudged each other down the line, tilting their cans knowingly.

He looked up, saw her and said, 'Oh, no.' They all laughed. They were just drunk cowboys out for a day's horseflesh judging. Unlike the other auction-goers, these hicks seemed to be here just to enjoy the spectacle. Some of them she recognised as the men she had spoken to earlier.

Maree said dully, 'You're not selling the horse. I'll die first.'

Ken said, 'I already have, pet—to a little old lady who'll only drive him on Sundays.' The other men guffawed. They were all old enough to be her father, older even. But then the driver looked at her with narrowed eyes and sat forward to put his beer down under the bench. 'You're real serious, for a girl,' he said.

A beery fellow with a paunch and a sunburned, cheerful face said, 'He's got his eye on you, sweetheart.'

Somebody else said, 'Yeah, his brown-eye.'

There was a general haw-haw but Ken didn't quite join in. He even sat up, looking at her as though assessing her worth.

'How much'd you give me to hold the horse?' he said suddenly.

She said coldly, 'I'd give you money if I had any, but I don't. My father might pay you something. Or how do you like the idea of gaol instead?'

Ken leaned back again so that his elbows rested on the tier behind him, comfortable among the boots of other men. Another fellow said wittily, 'He didn't mean money, sweetheart. He meant how much o' that!' He pointed at her breasts and chuckled noisily, tipping his can. Maree crossed her arms over her chest and tried to look curveless.

Another man leaned conversationally and said, 'It's a figure of speech, love. Hold your horse.' Squaring himself comically, he roared, 'Hello there, Miss, can I hold your horse?'

The brown-eye wit added, 'Yeah, sweetheart, he means how much'll you give him to ride you!' and she might even have flown at the lot of them, she was now so furious, only Ken was actually looking embarrassed, and he said to the final commentator, 'We don't need that, thanks, Barry. This girl's got a thing for one o' Winterson's animals, that's all. Reckons it's hers.'

Maree kept fighting the impossible battle of slandering a man in front of his mates. 'It *is* my horse, and you shouldn't have taken him,' she said, 'or haven't you heard of a thing called theft?'

The men all seemed to get bored; there was a general turning away. Ken said, with an undertone of kindness, 'Love, I don't believe that's your animal, but if the bid don't hit two hundred, I'll hang onto him 'cause it won't be worth me effort anyway, since I'm only getting twenty per cent. Not to mention if it's under that it'll be dogger.'

Cold inside now, she said, 'What?'

He shrugged. 'You know—dogger. Fella over there.'

A man in grey overalls sat by himself opposite the ring, hands on both knees, looking with interest at the crush that led into the corral. A whippety boy stood alongside him, leaning through the fence and conversing animatedly.

Ken said ruefully, 'That old buggar takes whatever he can get for a hundred—donkeys, twenty-year-olds, year-lings even, you name it. Takes 'em straight to the factory and they chop 'em up for cans of food for little fluffy poodles for girls like you.' He sat up with a sort of pride, seeing the look on her face. 'Don't worry, I never took a horse here I let go to the dogs, it's not me way.'

Maree sat on a tree stump, clearing it first of beer cans. If she'd had a bridle and saddle she'd go right back to the yard, which was not so well attended now that the auction was on, and saddle her horse up and ride him out of there like they did in Westerns. She glanced toward the saddlery tent and it, too, seemed unattended. Even a halter and lead rope, she thought, would make it possible to take the horse and go. She might not get far, and she might even fall off, but Ken and his truck wouldn't so easily go where a girl with a horse could, and nobody could easily catch him once he was out and about.

Or she could set him free. This would give her parents time to come, supposing they found out from Lissa where she was, supposing they *would* come.

With this last course of action in mind, she left the cowboys and went guiltily to the saddlery tent. Two stew-ards at the far end were discussing something on a sheet of paper. All she had to do was reach across the trestle tables and steal a bridle. But then she saw that everything not positioned out of reach was clipped to the trestle tables by a long thread of wire that ran through metal rings or through splits and gaps in the packaging. Even the cage of rabbits was tethered in this fashion. Anything in job lots, such as bunches of lead ropes, were clipped together and covered in plastic, so that if she wanted just one bridle she'd have to run away with a whole rustling package. Even so, she haunted the tables, reluctant to dismiss the plan, for it was all she had. What was strewn so rubbishlike across these tables was everything her life lacked: quality, craft, completion. The bridle and saddle she owned were both rotted and falling apart.

The saddles were all up on a portable wall mounting, too high for her to reach unless she made a spectacle of herself by standing on a table, but she stood quite a while looking at them just because her envy was so acute. A girl came in, svelte and black-clad, in calf-length riding boots and with her hair held back by a velvet headband. She was pink-cheeked, all English rose in an Australian desert, exuding money. She strode along with a grey-haired man and when she got near Maree, said, 'That one,' pointing to a black, straight-flapped saddle on the wall mount.

The man, who must have been her father, said, 'All right,' and called to the stewards to bring it closer so that he could inspect the seams.

Maree left the tent, her envy stronger than ever. She could have waited until the stewards and the English rose were engrossed in the show saddle, but the idea of theft no longer appealed. She went dispiritedly back to the corral and pushed her way through to the stump, which, because she was shorter than the men who had gathered in front, she was able to stand upon, not caring whose view she blocked. Looking about, it was all she could do not to kick perfect strangers in the backs of their moleskin-clad legs.

A stocky little petrol-drum of a pony was ridden into

the ring and the auctioneer rattled his voice through a loudspeaker. 'And lot number 20 is a little gem of a pony, guaranteed quiet, good to shoe, float, part Welsh Mountain and you can see his breeding papers here, got a good straight little walk, lovely paces, round he goes. Beanie, give us a little canter there, Beanie, nice kind eye, six-year-old, he's been in a dozen shows and, let me see, won first place in two events at last year's Royal, and what do we have to start a bid here, folks, do we have two hundred bid, at two hundred bid, do we have two hundred bid, yes we have two hundred dollars bid, we have two hundred bid, do we have two-fifty bid, yes we have two-fifty bid, no sir, we'll not take twenty at this stage, sir, two hundred-fifty bid, we have two hundred-fifty bid, at two-fifty, at two-fifty, we have three hundred, we have three hundred dollars bid, at three hundred dollars, we have three-fifty . . .'

Clinching this sale took about five minutes of hysterical bidding. A great many of the family buyers, mostly girls with their dads, left in disappointment after this, having obviously pinned their hopes on the one animal. Six or seven ponies, occasionally led around if they were not properly broken, came into the ring, were put through their paces, and generally sold. After about thirty minutes, a horse the exact style of Maree's grey, only bay in colour and better fed, went after lacklustre bidding for a hundred and five dollars. Maree saw the dogger raise his hand as the final bid and her heat sank. The saleyard steward nodded at the big dogger man in overalls, and without having to ask, jotted down his name. Maree had never felt her lack of purchasing power so acutely as in this transaction in which, had she had a mere hundred and ten dollars, she might have saved the animal's life.

She was conscious of somebody watching and saw Ken the driver giving her a curious look. Suddenly he leaned toward her, mouth pulled to one side. His eyes were a pallid aqua. He said, 'Tell you what. Say the nag does hit one-fifty, I get, what, thirty dollars, plus ten for handling and truckin' him. Don't hardly seem worth it, does it?'

Maree glared. Another, even bigger horse came through, well over sixteen hands, and for the moment she focussed on the animal being ridden through its paces. Nobody even made a bid until the dogger cut in just before the end and offered sixty dollars. She stood up, sickened and reeling. Then a few short bids began. Finally somebody in a far corner bought the horse for a hundred and ten. The dogger sat down to wait for the next. They were just scrub horses, she realised, big angular beasts ridden fast and hard over a couple of weeks for an education and then run through in a job-lot. Her own horse was no different to these; in fact, he probably would have ended up as dog food if she had not bought him right away.

The cowboy said, 'What I'm saying is, if you give me petrol money and another fifteen, I'll take him back to Winterson's and you can fight it out there. 'Cause, see, I still don't believe you got the right horse, but I don't reckon he'll be too happy if I take under one-fifty. It's just a bum day, is all.'

Maree said, 'Why are they going so cheap?' and the driver thought a while.

'Well,' he said, rubbing his chin, 'maybe it's a bad time for feed, and a big horse takes a lot of chaff. Maybe there's just nobody here after a stock horse. Most of these people know what they want, I guess.'

'Have you ever bought a horse here?' she asked, and he baulked and said hotly, 'No way! Auctions are for know-it-alls and first-timers. Y' always end up with some-body else's bad trainin'.' He shook his head sadly, but it was impossible to tell if he was serious.

After a while, Maree said, 'So can you ride?' Shouts and hoofbeats in the dust told her another sale was going through. The auctioneer finished every deal with, 'Righty-ho!' before he banged the hammer.

'I grew up on horseback,' he said. 'Me dad ran cows years ago. We always had 'em.'

Just then a gasp of awe went up and a beautiful Appaloosa stallion, crested and prancing at the end of a show lead, entered the ring. The auctioneer said, 'Well, folks, here's what you came for, a real chance at getting y'self one of the cleanest, finest stallions this side o' the States.'

Maree was a girl at a rodeo without any prospects and without cash. Vacantly she said, 'My dad'll pay the fifteen. I haven't got any money on me. We just want our horse back.'

Ken nodded but did not move. He was riveted on the corral. The other men were nudging each other and saying, 'He's a real type, isn't 'e?'

BJ Loudspeaker drew in his breath. He seemed able to talk for minutes on end without pausing for air. 'What am I bid for this superb Appaloosa stallion, four-year-old, out of Marshall's Pride by Son of a Gun, fifteen and a half hands, as you see he's just reached show condition and ready for the ring, he's already won reserve champion at last year's Easter Show and I believe he's destined for great things either as stud or western pleasure . . .'

Maree was standing by Ken's knee, looking at him in despair. The force of her scrutiny too much, he glanced at her, seemed to blanch, and murmured, 'Come on.' As he got up, he tipped his nonexistent hat at the men around and those who were not fixated on the horse tipped theirs back. Maree glanced into the ring once more, and waited to watch the beautiful spotted animal. He was like something out of a book, a statue of a horse, big barrelled, muscular, arched and spring-loaded, each creamy movement an essay in coordination—a dream of a horse.

The bidding started at three thousand dollars.

Maree caught up with Ken down near the main holding yard. He had stopped on his way to say hello to acquaintances, and while he was having a word to somebody she studied her horse through the rails. He was standing in a far corner, lower lip drooping and hind leg resting on its tip. The ewe neck with the shorn mane could not be disguised, nor could the lean hindquarters or shabby hips. This was a horse that needed feeding and careful exercise to build up muscle, and still he would never be a beautiful horse.

Even so, a new hope had hatched. If she arrived home with the horse, she might be forgiven for having run away. Hers was not the sort of family to collapse in relief around a runaway, shedding grateful tears. Hers was the sort of family to box the ears of the errant. Without the horse, she was doomed.

A heavy-set man strode up to Ken. 'These old bags o' bones aren't going for much, eh?' he said cheerily.

Ken said, 'Oh, I wouldn't say that.'

'How much you reckon he'll get?' the large man asked.

Having climbed through the fence to pat her horse, Maree scurried back with a vague cry.

'That depends,' Ken said. 'What y' want him for?'

'Tell the truth, I train pacers. Some o' me best runners

came from knackeries. This horse's got the right shape, though he's not much t' look at right now.'

Ken said, 'I'll give 'im to you for two hundred.'

'Argh, y' got saddle-sores on y' head, mate. One-twenty. You're already ahead of auction.'

'One-eighty. I pulled 'im out of sale for this girl, see? Only she hasn't got the cash on her so we haven't shook hands.'

Maree called out, 'Pig! Liar!' She was afraid of both of them, and danced around at a distance like a pup around brawling dogs. If only she had a gun, a truck, a bank account of her own. She did not even have a few cents to call the police, and her parents were out combing the suburb so that they could punish her when they found her. If only her mother and her father would become the sort of parents who understood a girl's deepest wish, and turned up to rescue her.

They were not.

The man said, 'Argh, y're killin' me. One sixty-five.'

They ignored her completely. They shook hands and cash came out of a wallet and went into Ken's back pocket, where it formed a bulge. The man had his own receipt book, which he passed across for Ken to sign. When Ken looked at his copy, he said, 'Listen, mate, I could deliver him for another ten. I got a truck up front.'

But the new owner held his hand up and said, 'I got me own float, mate. Just give me ten minutes, there's one more lot I want to bid on, eh? D' y' mind?' He obviously knew Ken by reputation, for he was happy to leave the horse with him for the time being.

'No problem,' Ken said, and the buyer sauntered off.

Ken got the money out to do some maths; he also appeared to be doctoring the receipt copy with the man's biro, which he had retained. Maree felt she was watching the work of a master criminal, and her a mere nobody. A girl with silly dreams. Cowboys, horses, men were there to stamp on them.

SIXTEEN

Maree wandered through the crowd. It surprised her that she did not feel like crying. She just felt absent. There were no phones. There were no friendly faces. There were only the indifferent or mildly curious glances of people with their own lives and their own purchasing power, their mortgages, their spare wheels, their back-hoes, their chickens, their ruptured barbed-wire fences, their ride-ons with missing parts. Maree saw the man who had bought her horse sitting with a beer in his hand beside the auction corral. She wanted to punch him in his fat ribs.

On the ground at her feet was a bit of hay-string. She stared at it vacantly, then, with a dawning sense of possibility, she picked it up.

She ran to the holding yard. Ken was in conversation with a muscular, haunchy woman in a checked shirt and jodhpurs. The woman had a punched-looking nose and squinty eyes, and kept laughing flirtatiously at what he said.

There was nobody at the corral gate, just as she had hoped.

Maree sneaked into the corral on the other side of the horse to Ken and the woman. Approaching the horse quietly, she rubbed his cartilaginous nose. He nibbled her palm. She looped the hay-string around his throat. His ears swivelled back and forth, but he walked forward without hesitation when she tugged the string. For once he was completely compliant. Nobody had seen her thus far. Maree got all the way to the gate. The chain was unpadlocked, merely looped through the timbers.

Maree opened the gate.

Nobody stopped her. Passers-by merely glanced at her, assuming she had bought the thing, and walked on.

The horse auction was almost over. Spectators were beginning to drift up toward the tack tent, where there was a good deal to go through, or down to the tractors and implements to do a bit of picking through. A few stragglers glanced at the hay-string around the horse's neck and gave Maree a sympathetic look.

At the top gate, the steward Maree had approached upon entering the saleyard was sitting on a black stump doing a crossword. Horses were being put onto trucks at the rear of the yards. She stopped and considered trying to take the horse past the steward, perhaps pretending that Ken had given him back to her. Then the steward looked up and Maree knew from the expression on his face that this would be no easy task. She would probably need a sale ticket or something, if she was not putting the horse on a float.

The grey stamped his big hoof. His eyes were so large they were like the giant tom marbles boys fought for, large and quizzical and full of equine gentleness. Maree turned him awkwardly, trying not to lose the joined ends of string, and went around the sale corral, away from the crowd. A few straggly horses were locked into side yards awaiting their collectors. She was looking for the truck entrance, where livestock carriers moved between parking lot and loading ramps; she thought she could convince one of these carriers to transport her horse as well, as long as they would accept payment at the other end, or else it might be possible to slip through the gate. But when she located the truck entrance, she saw another steward hanging about with a clickboard.

She knew she would be caught.

Maree steered the grey horse into an empty yard and tied the gate with the hay-string. If she was lucky, nobody would notice him for a short time. Then she went back to where she could see Ken, still talking to the woman in the checked shirt. As she watched, he glanced over his shoulder and saw the empty corral. He did a sort of double-take and checked his watch. At the same time, the man who had bought the horse came down the hill from the saleyard, scratching his head.

Maree hurried to the exit. There was no way to take the horse out without being spotted. Still, he might remain unseen in the small yard just long enough for her to call home. In the depths of misery she almost convinced herself her father would listen and be sympathetic. All he had to do was drive their idiotic pink-doored car or send the police.

She ran down the road until she came to the street with the service station. Out of breath, she staggered under the carport. The orange-haired man was dipping a long stick into steel-lidded holes in the ground; he stood up and said, 'It's the phone again, I'll bet,' as she approached. After a few more unhurried dippings, he wiped his hands on a blackened rag and turned on his heel toward the shop. She followed meekly. This time he rang the operator and handed her the phone, to ensure, she thought, that the charge truly was reversed. Once more, he loitered while she spoke.

Her father came on the line. Maree could hear the operator saying, 'Is that an accept, do you accept the call?'

Her father said, 'That depends!'

'Is that yes or no?'

'Yes,' he said after a long pause, 'I will accept the call.'

The line cleared. Maree said, 'Dad?'

He gave a grunt of acknowledgement. In the background her mother was saying, 'Is she all right? Where is she?'

Maree said, 'Dad, I'm at an auction. They took the horse in a truck, so I jumped on as well, because there was this dog—'

He interrupted as though he had not heard a word of her story. 'There are only two words we need to hear from you,' he said. 'Can you guess what those are?'

Maree said, 'Please, Dad—'

'Two words,' he went on in his steely, unforgiving voice. 'Two words: "I'm sorry." Or even, "I'm sorry to cause so much trouble, Dad." Or a combination of words, "I'm sorry I'm not still at home and I'm coming home right now."'

When they had briefly owned the dog, Maree's father had once stooped to pet the thing. Rolled over on his back, Mr Pyjama had urinated up in the air in thin spurts. Their father had chortled in disgust and wiped his hands.

Maree thought she understood the abject grin of the

dog as he wet himself: authority was ludicrous. But it was also real.

She felt her face growing red from anger. Heat suffused each pore. Her hands sweated. 'Dad,' she pleaded one more time, 'I'm just trying to get my horse back.'

There was another long pause. Then he said, 'The horse is not the point, Maree. We're in a new league now. We're in the league of kids who run away from home. And do you know what that means?'

'No.'

'That means,' he said in a droning voice, 'that until you get yourself back here, in my house, in my sight, that horse doesn't matter. Doesn't exist. I will not do anything to help. If you come home within an hour, then fine, by all means we'll go to the police station and we'll make a report. Let the police handle it. But until you get your face in this front door, my girl, you're on your own, and I mean that.'

He hung up. Maree's father had never hung up on her before; this was truly the worst of his brutish acts.

The orange-haired man, looking the other way, had his hand out for the receiver. As she passed it across, he said, 'Home trouble?' His tattoos were littered with wiry hairs like miniature orange springs.

Maree nodded so savagely she grew dizzy. Perhaps the oxlike man with tattoos would adopt her.

He shrugged and stepped backward.

Back at the auction yards, horse trucks were coming and going, revving up and slowing down, bucking over ruts and reversing to park. Men whirled lassos over their heads, sitting on open tailgates. Girls hugged their own arms in the shadows of station wagons, idly smoking cigarettes. A few low-slung motorbikes with handlebar ends dangling streamers exactly like Lissa's dragster leaned in a pack, waiting for their riders to return. For the first time, looking at the motorbikes, Maree had an inkling of what it was these men and girls saw in the noisy machines, for it was somehow similar to what she wanted in her horse.

She strode on, into the fray. The yard where she had left the grey was, predictably, empty, the hay-string broken on the ground. She walked listlessly now, skirting the few remaining horses, watching as each was loaded onto a truck or roped and led. Her eyes were too tired to cry.

A double horse float was parked at the end of the series of corrals. Tied to this was the grey horse; standing nearby was Ken, keeping guard.

Maree went right up to him, hands on her hips.

He said, 'Thought you had 'im there, eh girl? Well, y' can't fool Ken.'

She said, 'Thief.'

'Are you always this suspicious?'

'Pig. Thief. Go to hell.'

He laughed. 'Might see y' there,' he said, and then, almost kindly, 'What's your name?'

'Maree Grace Sterry. If it's anything to you.'

'Well, Maree Grace Sterry, you nearly done me a bad turn,' he said. 'But I guess we'll leave it there, eh. Got the guy his horse back. Wasn't too well hid, actually.'

Maree said, 'The police are just walking in the top gate now. They've got machine guns.'

Despite himself, he checked. Then he laughed again. 'You just don't give up,' he said. 'You're like one of them pig dogs—what are they?—bull terriers.' His voice almost had a fondness in its tone.

'I wish I was, so I could bite you in pieces.' She went to the grey and stroked his muzzle, making small throaty whispers of goodbye. His bottom lip drooped and his eyelids with their tufty fringe almost closed.

'Where's the fat guy?' she asked indifferently.

'He went to buy a couple o' harnesses and a raggy little yearling. He thinks you're with me, see, my little sister or something. At least that's what I said so he wouldn't get you arrested. Don't care much for cops myself.'

Maree said, 'That figures,' and he laughed again.

'You're too much,' he said, 'but I'm glad you're not me little sister, 'cause I'd have to give you a whupping. Smack smack, over me knee.'

'I wouldn't care if I was arrested. I've been kicked out of home now, thanks to you. I've got no horse any more; you've sold him. Gaol couldn't be worse than that, could it?'

The cowboy looked at her curiously again, and he rubbed a hand on his brow. 'Come on, I'll take you home,' he said sheepishly. 'Your parents'll see reason. I'd never leave a girl in trouble.'

'As if I'd trust you.'

He shrugged and said, 'Whoop—here he comes. Your fat guy, I mean.'

Maree looked up. The man was leading a shaggy-maned, leggy yearling, and he started when he saw her. The young boy who had earlier in the day mouthed off about the appy was stumbling along indifferently behind the man, carrying a heap of leather and buckles. They both scowled at one another and then at Ken.

Maree turned back to the horse. He had chosen this moment to stamp at a fly, and his forehoof caught just the edge of her toe, through her shool shoe, pinching it to the earth. Her face contorted as she tried to reef her foot away.

Then the big grey raised his head and performed a great, wide-mouthed yawn.

Maree, looking into the depths of his mouth, among the great grassy tongue and knobbly teeth, saw, just behind the large, yellow-rimmed incisors, the tusk of a long, curved bridle-tooth, absent from an ordinary three-year-old, certainly absent from the mouth she had seen at purchase.

This horse was at least a five-year-old and probably older. He was not hers at all.

He lifted his hoof and she cleared her pained foot and limped a little away from the horse float, clutching an inward shock. She was cursing, crying, wincing, and trying not to catch Ken's eye in case he saw in her expression the same thing she had seen.

Ken watched her walk off and, waving to the heavy-set man, followed her into the shade of a grove of skinny eucalypts, where she sat on a log. Her toe throbbed. She was crying, but then her dejection gave way to laughter. Maree rocked back and forth, howling, crying and laughing at once.

The driver studied her for some time, then he sat on the log next to her.

'Maree Grace Sterry,' he said, 'you sure are weird.' Then he put his arm around her shoulders.

When she stiffened, he sat a little apart from her and began to toy with a small stick, breaking pieces off and hurling them into the distance. Maree was shuddering with stifled giggles. At last the spasms eased.

Ken was looking at her curiously. One of his hands, she realised, was sitting on top of her knee, and she was horrified to see the index finger moving backward and forward, softly stroking.

Jennifer Kremmer

To stop the flow of this moment, which contained its own vast threat, she blurted, 'You're right. He's not my horse.'

Ken didn't even blink. He said, 'Of course he ain't. What do you think I am, a thief?'

He began to laugh. Then he slapped her knee and stood up, shaking his head. 'I gotta deliver some hay,' he said, 'and if you'd like to come along I can get you on home afterward.'

Maree, standing, said, 'Yeah. Whatever.'

SEVENTEEN

Ken drove toward her home suburb after several detours to pick up and deliver. They rumbled into a feed store, collected a great many sacks of chaff and bales of hay, and circled back toward the auction, even driving right past the entranceway. The motorbikes had swelled ranks and were now festooned with ancient-looking men in leather vests and deep brown beards; girls in three-quarter pants and midriff tops hung about or looped their arms over the men's necks. Maree stared almost wistfully at them, craning until they were out of sight. They were like different creatures to her—another culture from another place. The rest of the auction yard looked to be nearing empty.

They pulled into a white-shacked hobby farm where a woman in an apron and spotted dress was scraping mash from a plate for a clucking flock of chickens. She wiped her forehead and waved Ken amicably to a feed shed. Brown and white cows tipped back their heads and lowed at her from behind barbed wire. Maree stayed in the truck while

Ken worked, absently watching the woman. She looked impossibly blonde; there was something artificial about her manner and dress. A singleted man came around from behind the shed and began to help Ken pile up the bales. When the woman glanced at Maree, Maree ducked. She did not want to speak to anybody.

Ken whistled as he worked and stood around a little longer chatting to the man. The woman stood back to watch them. Her posture suggested such capability to Maree—such a world of difference, actually—that she wanted, there and then, to be turned into a replica of this stranger, an adult, a woman in the world. Maree would live on her own farm, with her own horses—and a man, perhaps like Ken. She would grow into a spotted dress and feed chooks.

What else was there to grow into?

She hunched in the seat and was both relieved and sorry when Ken returned, wearing a startled expression and a layer of chaff dust. She remembered that he had touched her at the auction. The memory made her blush.

He climbed into the truck and started it, then said, 'You know, you're kind of pretty, when you're not runnin' after horses and gettin' all worked up. Come to think of it,' he shoved the truck into gear, 'you're not so bad looking when you're angry, either. Like a little filly, all fired up.'

Her blush turned brickish.

Ken drove lightly, one arm out the window. He kept laughing and shaking his head while she tried to describe how similar the horse was to her own. Finally, he said, 'I didn't think you could be that sure. Half a day isn't enough, not unless you're a horse y'self, in which case, like I always say, they're as different apart as you and me.'

Maree started to say, 'He just looks so much like my

horse,' but the words 'my horse' sounded so silly that she stopped. There was no evidence that she had ever had one. Perhaps everything up to the horse's escape had been a particularly vivid dream.

Now she was going to have a particularly vivid awakening. The thought of walking in her front door alarmed her unutterably. Driving along in the cowboy's truck reminded her of dreams in which she was falling through space, knowing that ahead was an inevitable jolt. As long as she kept falling, she was relatively safe.

The stitching on her jeans was coming undone over her calf. To hide this, she crossed her legs. In the same instant she realised that she had to go to the toilet, and all manner of physical dramas began playing themselves out in her body: her nipples had begun to sting where they rubbed against the cloth of her shirt; her back ached; there was a red weal she had no memory of having caused on the skin above her hand. Maree felt hot and cold by turns, and her teeth were chattering.

Ken was nonchalant, and whistled as they drove. He bought her a hamburger when he stopped for petrol at a service station, a truckie-haunt about five kilometres from the beginnings of suburbia. She was too keyed-up to eat, and only managed to nibble around the edges of saucy lettuce, rejecting the meat, while reassuring him she'd pay him back. She'd never been able to eat in front of unfamiliar, or even partly familiar, boys—nor, of course, men. Eating reminded her too much of other functions of her body, such as her budding femininity, shit and piss and odour.

But Ken had no trouble wrapping his face around his hamburger, and even expressed an interest in finishing hers off, which both relieved and somewhat disgusted Maree;

she was sick of holding it and feeling the juices dribbling down her arm.

She tried not to watch him eat, since he did it so organically, opening his throat like a snake. In fact, his eating did not so much repulse as fascinate, and if anything it was her own fascination that she found repulsive.

Maree half wanted to be home in bed, where she could think about the cowboy, if she liked, or anything to avoid thinking about her horse.

The horse that she had thought was her horse.

Perhaps there was no horse at all.

The back of the truck rattled emptily in the summer wind. When they reached Maree's suburb, she half-heartedly gazed out of the window. She'd been out all day. It was almost dark and the streetlights were on. Maree saw nothing remotely resembling the horse she had lost, and in fact she was not really looking. Every now and then, whistling, the cowboy sneaked a coy glance in her direction.

A kilometre or so from her house, Ken pulled the truck over, saying he'd heard an odd noise. He got out, lifted the big dusty bonnet and stayed there for a few minutes, to make the ploy realistic. Then he climbed in again, but something in his face was different.

It was the first time anyone had ever kissed her. A man-to-girl kiss, that is. Or even boy-to-girl.

She had had no time to think about whether she wanted to be kissed. It just happened. She sat primly upright, in great shock, feeling her mouth attempt to make the appropriate response.

Worrying about doing it properly stopped her from fighting off the kiss. The fact of a man's mouth on hers was insubstantial compared to her deep phobia about offending him. She wanted to seem like a girl who kissed routinely, who had experience. She felt the pressure of lips on lips, the startling closeness of another face, and a liquidy melting around her mouth, but these were purely physical sensations. She was overwhelmed by a fear of failing.

Ken's arm reached around her waist, then slid upward until he found a breast. He gave it a tentative squeeze. She half thought that at any moment he would sit back in alarm and say, 'My, they are unusual bosoms.' Having no idea of what was supposed to occur in or around her breast, she arched her ribcage so that she would be in easy reach. Nothing seemed to matter, for he casually moved on.

He murmured in her ear in the briefest of respites from kissing, 'Mmmm, baby, you're a natural.' His words struck her as unreal; she kept wanting to laugh. Then a motile agony came and went in her lower stomach and she flinched.

He shifted so that the gear-stick was not blocking so much of his upper body, and more of his tense and skinny torso in the flannelette shirt pressed against her. He murmured again, thick phrases familiar from books or movies. 'Mmmm, baby, you have sweet little lips, sugar honey,' or, 'Get a little closer, kid, I won't bite.' And indeed he lied in this, for his teeth approached the curve of her throat near the jugular and she gasped a little at the sucking pressure he applied.

Maree was entirely unprepared for anything like this. Finally, she pulled away. She sat upright and he looked surprised. 'Sweet sixteen and never had a hickey?' he asked, reaching for his ignition switch.

Maree swallowed in gulps.

She was so astonished that a man could go from sucking her throat to the steering column in one swift manoeuvre that she said primly, 'Let me out here—I'll walk. It's just a few blocks ahead.'

He said, 'Nah, it's okay. Home it is, eh?'

Just before they reached her house, he slowed right down, preparing to drop her where she pointed, two houses away from hers, but he grew distracted and sailed along the kerb until they were virtually at the front gate. He waited for her to clamber out, and when she hesitated to see if he would say anything or do anything as a parting gesture, he began whistling and wiping at the windshield with a handkerchief as though nothing at all had happened in the truck.

Maree said, hiding disappointment behind courtesy, 'Thanks for the lift,' and slammed the door. Her throat and face were pulsing with an intimate heat, and with a rush of horror she knew intuitively that one of the kisses had left a mark on her throat.

The truck, idling, was thrust into gear. Maree caught a final glimpse of Ken as he began to move, and half expected him to wink, but he merely tipped his hand to his forehead and drove off.

Then everything melted into the growl of a throat being cleared from the porch. Maree sensed the shifting of something to a reality so here-and-now she no longer even heard the truck. She walked up the verandah steps in a circle of light cast from the television, in which her father stood, his arms crossed upon his chest, gazing out in a way that suggested he had no idea that she had arrived home.

Yet he was blocking the front doorway, an overgrown boy of a man, waiting for her to make the first move.

'Dad, I—' she began, and he held up one hand, palm out, a gesture not of peace but of silence. Then he gave her three hard, though measured, whacks across the face.

Each time he swung, he made a little intro, and after the blow landed, a reason. 'That,' *slap*, 'is for worrying your mother. And that,' *slap*, 'is for running off with some stranger who could've been a maniac. And that,' *slap*, 'is for losing your horse in the first place.'

At each slap, her horizon, a row of bricks in shadow against the spilled lounge-room light, dizzied itself and then righted in a slightly different hue.

Her father ordered her with his thumb into the house, in which the rest of her family, mute, hovered in shadows with their mouths sealed. It was understood she was not allowed to say anything, and she knew with the less dizzy parts of her brain that had she so much as murmured, waves of shouting would have fallen on her head.

Maree did not need to be told to go to her room. All she wanted to do was lie on her bed, the one position in the home that was solely hers. When her father went past a minute or two later, he said, 'And you can leave the door open, Miss, so we know you're there.'

She collapsed into her pillow, devoid even of tears. The cottony pillowcase smelled of lemon laundry detergent and sunny air. It was a case of lies. Maree hurled her pillow across the room, and put her face on her bare arms.

After a while Lissa came to the room, inching cautiously. She stood near the doorway, every now and then peering to either side down the hall. Her posture was difficult to interpret, and her face was closed. Maree might have shouted at her and destroyed their girlhood link, or she might have uttered to her some damnation of their father and condemned them both; she was quite beyond caring about what happened next.

Lissa slowly drew the door shut and crept closer.

'Dad says I can't talk to you, Face-ache,' she began.

Then a giggle burst from her and she threw herself face-down onto Maree's sheet. Each time she lifted her head to say something, she dissolved. By her third or fourth out-burst, Maree could not hold back a chortle herself. Then they were mutually hysterical, rolling from side to side, tears trickling out of aching eyes. Lissa fell backward to the floor and split her best boob tube, and after that neither of them had any hope of becoming sober. They stuffed their mouths with bedclothes or their fists, and tried to keep one eye on the bedroom door while they doubled up in spasms. But nobody else heard them or came in.

Maree awoke in the middle of the night with a strange feeling in her lower abdomen, just above the pubic bone. It was softer than a stab but more painful than an ache. She could not locate its source.

The house around her was quiet and dark. She stared at the flickers of occasional traffic illuminating the ceiling above her bed, and listened to the noises the house made as it slept. A clock ticked. Lissa let out a soft snore.

She was thinking about the experience of being kissed. Instead of the feeling of the cowboy's mouth on hers, however, she remembered a fluttery tremble in her lower belly as his hand had brushed her hip. And then she remembered that he had bitten her on the neck. Of all things to come home with, she had brought a bite-mark.

Her hand moved absently to her thigh, where a sticky feeling made the inner surfaces feel chafed. In a pale sliver of streetlight, she saw the blackness on her fingers, and in a numb sort of shock let herself quietly out of the bedroom to go to the bathroom.

In the silent mirror the blood on her hand matched the brand on her neck from the cowboy's bite.

Maree felt the creep of humours from the lower half of

her body, and almost expected to faint, but nothing happened.

Standing at the bathroom mirror, remembering the cowboy's kiss, she put her hand to her face. It was warm.

EIGHTEEN

Maree was not allowed out of her room, except to eat and visit the bathroom, for three days. While she was locked in, Lissa kindly went around the neighbourhood distributing a hand-drawn leaflet that she had made several copies of, using up spare paper from school exercise books.

Three days after the horse had run off, two sheepish boys turned up on the doorstep and said through the screen door, 'Is this the house where the girl lost a grey horse?'

Maree's mother said, 'Yes. Why?'

'We've got him. He's at our place, in the carport.'

Maree's mother asked for their address with a tone of indifference. She said, 'We'll be in touch.'

The boys flicked a hand-ball as they left the porch.

Maree's mother stood in her doorway, hands on her hips, biting her lip. Lissa had gone roller-skating; there was only Samantha, her mother and Maree in the house.

'I don't know what your father would say,' she said quietly, not looking at Maree. Then her expression changed.

'Did something happen to you that I should know about, Maree?' she asked.

Maree thought she meant the kiss in the truck. Guiltily, she said, 'No.' She put a hand to her neck to hide the mark.

'Are you sure?' Her mother was not quite looking at Maree, her eyes kept skipping over the room.

'Why should anything have happened?'

'If it's what I think it is,' her mother went on, 'then I suppose you'll be needing something for it. Something from the chemist, I mean.'

Maree expelled a breath. 'Oh, that,' she said. 'Lissa gave me some of her tampons.' She said 'tampons' very quickly, hiding the sound, afraid of what it meant.

Her mother nodded in relief and started smoothing the front of her dress. She seemed embarrassed. 'Let's go get the horse then,' she said breezily, 'then you'll have to come back to your room. When Dad gets home we'll see if he'll let you out to feed and water it.'

Maree said, 'I bet he says no.' But her mother was already walking off down the hall.

They found the horse ten minutes away, where the boys had walked him after finding him near the reserve. He was roped up beside a palm-groved fibro house, beneath a rusty awning. Several strands of the rope had been knotted about each awning leg. The horse was standing with his head drooped to a yellow plastic bucket of water. He was paler than the horse she had chased across the suburbs, with fewer flecks. He looked like a skeleton or ghost.

'Phantom,' she called, and the animal turned. It was as good a name as any for a horse.

Mrs Sterry let Maree do the talking. The boys were playing marbles in the shade of the three-step porch. They said gloomily, 'We were going to keep him but Dad wouldn't let us.'

Inside the carport, with the aid of bread, it was an easy matter to slide the bridle over the horse's head, and Maree even felt she had some expertise buckling up the throat-latch while the horse chewed. Her mother helped her undo the ropes fencing him in, keeping Samantha out of the way with a backward hand.

'Thanks,' Maree said, and waved a little grudgingly at the boys. They did not get up.

Her mother walked on one side with Samantha, keeping the younger girl well out of the way of the animal's hooves. A tea-towel hung over one of her shoulders, and she squinted at the sun as though not ordinarily permitted such excursions. Maree held the reins firmly behind the horse's chin, and, perhaps chastened by his experience at the boys' house, the horse plodded quietly. The swish of his tail occasionally stung her legs. She did not care at all that he was hers.

When they got to the side yard, her mother stood behind her, and the instant the horse was inside the gate she closed it. Now named, Phantom put his head down and began to snatch at grass. Maree filled a bucket with water, left him to drink and went back into her room. She did not want to watch or pat him—this surprised her most of all.

At six o'clock their father came home. Lissa had sneaked a packet of hair dye out of a chemist's shop and, having closed their bedroom door, was showing Maree the colour. It looked exactly the same as her own hair. She was wearing a pink boob tube under a black and white Japanese robe, and pink polished cotton pants with a black belt. Maree looked at her sister and felt awed; there was something in Lissa's ability to concoct herself out of clothing that simultaneously caused envy and disdain. When they heard the front door close, they both sat up and stared at each other in mock terror, Lissa dragging both hands down her cheeks and whispering grandly, 'Oh, dear God protect us!' Footsteps sounded in the hall, a door was opened, a pair of socks was flung. They heard murmurs behind walls. Their mother called Lissa out to set the table for dinner, and just before she left she tucked the hair dye sachet into a rolled towel and made the sign of the cross. Then she stopped to listen at the door.

'Sounds like he's off his high horse,' she said, giving Maree a wry look as she opened the door.

At six-thirty Maree was called out to eat. She kept her head low, spooning the potato mash and green beans, and out of habit alone toying with the rissoles. When her mother gave her a sharp glance, she hurriedly ate them too.

After dinner she went back to the bedroom. Lissa went into the bathroom to perform chemical reactions upon her hair.

Maree brushed her own hair, looking in the dresser mirror for some exterior sense of herself—as she supposed Lissa was able to see herself. Was Maree really pretty? What was pretty? What did the cowboy mean? Unlike Lissa, she never bought magazines, except equine ones. Maree turned her face this way and that, seeing only eyes, eyes seeing eyes, eyes pretending to be other than herself for the purposes of scrutiny.

She was either beautiful or ugly or some combination thereof. It was impossible to tell.

Her father stuck his head around the door. 'Maree,' he said in a tone of indifference that was meant to remind her of the magnitude of her crime, 'you are allowed out of your room, long as you keep yourself in sight. The minute you leave the house, for anything at all, without asking explicit permission, you go back into your room. Understood? And that includes to feed the horse.'

She said, 'Thanks, Dad,' with an undercurrent of sarcasm so subtle it failed to invoke the usual spark. Her father gave a short look and left.

She threw the hairbrush onto Lissa's bed and followed him.

Samantha was sitting on the lounge-room floor, clapping her hands in time with something on the television. 'Maree's here!' she cried, getting to her feet and running to hug her older sister's waist.

Touched a little, Maree swung her in the air.

Their mother cried, 'Careful. Don't knock the table leg!' She was stooped and gluing the lever of Mr Sterry's recliner back to its stub. He was sitting at the dining table reading the paper. Every now and then they heard his chair scrape upon the tiles.

Mrs Sterry finished gluing, put the tube away and went to set up her sewing machine.

Maree fetched the saddle and sat on the floor rubbing colourless shoe wax into it, trying to coax a bit of health into the ancient leather. Tomorrow, begging permission of course, she would ride the horse around his yard. When she got accustomed to him and he to Maree, she would take him to the park. Once, these plans would have excited her tremendously, but now she just felt duty-bound to see them through.

Her father walked in. Ignoring Maree, he sat in his usual chair and unthinkingly reached down to adjust the lever. It came off in his hand.

Samantha squealed, 'Mummy, Daddy broke the chair again!'

He snorted in his throat and put the broken piece on the floor beside him. He had not yet condescended to recognise Maree in common spaces. This meant he could not turn to his second eldest, even in surprise or consternation, and it also meant that she was at liberty to smirk at Sam's remark. Mrs Sterry, craning around from her sewing position, called out, 'I didn't think the glue was quite dry yet, dear.'

Mr Sterry hunkered down, hands loose over the chair's arms. He did not reply.

When she had finished rubbing the wax into its creaky leather, Maree left the saddle on a heap of newspaper in the corner of the lounge room, close to the Christmas tree. This very action reminded Samantha of things presenty, for she sat up straight and said to Maree, 'Guess what, Maree, Santa's coming soon.'

Involuntarily, they all looked at their father. He had given up on the television and was sitting with his head back in the chair, arms loose at his sides. 'Not now, Samantha,' said their mother. 'Come and get ready for bed.'

The girl protested, but was led into the bedroom, where Maree heard her muffled squeals give way to low giggles as her mother, sewing aside, began a long-forgotten ritual nightly tickle.

From the man in the recliner rocker came a low, furtive snore.

Just then, Lissa came out of the bathroom to show off her new colour rinse. Her blonde hair looked exactly the same as usual to Maree, except that the ends seemed fainter and more wispy, even split.

Nevertheless, she said, 'That looks great. Really. It does.'

Lissa said, 'You know, Maree, I've just realised how like Dad you look.'

Maree shook her head. 'I don't look like anybody. I'm an orphan. I was adopted. Mum just told me yesterday.'

'Nuh-uh,' Lissa said firmly. 'You take after Dad. I take after Mum.'

At that point, Maree's mother stopped by the doorway and looked from one daughter to the other. Her cheeks drooped and in the yellow lounge room light she seemed small, as though in the new festive season she had developed a gift-giver's slouch. Yet when anybody in the family thought of generosity, they imagined a red-suited fat man with a beard.

She said, 'Shouldn't that television be turned off? Are either of you girls getting ready for bed?' Before they could answer, she suddenly sprang forward in a nervous swoop. 'Who's had my cigarettes?' They were parked on the edge of Lissa's manicure chair.

Lissa lied, 'Nobody, Mum.' She had taken one with her when she went to the shop for hair colorant and smoked it while chatting to a boy from school. It was just one of the things she sometimes did, like dyeing her hair.

Mr Sterry snuffled and in mixed relief and dread they all turned. He had drifted sideways, head propped against the headrest. At this angle his forehead was lined and weary and he looked ten years older than usual.

Perhaps to distract her mother from cigarettes, Lissa said, 'Watch this.' She tiptoed toward the sideboard, manicured nails curved over into pretend talons. Maree and her mother watched as, feather duster in hand, she leaned over their father's sleeping form. 'Dare me?' she whispered witch-like across the room.

Maree whispered, 'Pshaw', not believing even her sister had the gall.

Mrs Sterry intoned, 'No, don't do that,' but she lit a cigarette, and sat on a chair's arm with her legs crossed.

'I dare myself then,' said Lissa. She moved the duster right across her father's face so that the feather-tips brushed very lightly, once, twice and three times. At this assault the man's nose twitched. For a moment Mrs Sterry and her daughters were captivated by the sight of Mr Sterry's jerking fingers, loose at the end of his long knuckles, and the tense workings beneath his facial skin. It was as though they'd never actually studied him before.

Then the horse in the yard outside, or the phantom of a horse, whatever he was, neighed, and some sense or knowledge of their father told Maree and Lissa he was going to wake. They stepped backward in a flurry. Mrs Sterry flung her smile behind her hand and her gaze upon the curtain rings.

'Oi,' said the patriarch, eyeing them, 'what are you lot up to?'

Lissa already had the feather duster tucked behind her back. She said, 'What do you mean, Dad?'

Maree held up her saddle polishing cloth and mimed a few last strokes, even though the saddle was in the corner.

Mrs Sterry raised her shoulders in a volcanic shrug. 'Nothing,' she said airily, 'just making wigwams for goose's bridals.' She stubbed her cigarette out in a mug and headed for the sewing table.

Jennifer Kremmer

The man looked from one girl to another across the room. His mouth seemed stuck open or else he was merely still half in dream.

'Never mind,' he said.

STA	Flight Center
S-Lon (Seoul) 17th June $1257. Korean air	

● <u>Subiaco</u> (15th Jan)

King

All Twin / Double

Room 2 $400 TV/Avd, lounge, Internet / computer usag

R3 $400 Sames above

R5 $300 TV/DVD Player

R8 $300 Internet / (comp. usage cupstairs)

Service $100 per person

$20 keyholder

Min 4 Weeks

Kirsty   9228 9008 or 0403 776

21/2
● Gary $290 a week
    1min to mt. Lawley

8/2
● Room for rent $125 a week — Dian

No bond / furn / Internet

Sms Ray   0448976197

● 31/12
   2 storey /Study / Berwick St.
       $165 Shem 0433283306
   all inc.

15/2
1 Zone
$120 inc enspenses
Oak st. train st
4 bed house

0411 729 509 Linda